Born in Galway in 1920, Eilis Dillon has written over forty books, published in several languages including Irish, English, French, Flemish, German, Polish, Czech, Icelandic, Swedish, Hebrew and Italian. Her six novels and many children's books, on a wide variety of subjects, had already won her numerous distinctions and a widespread critical reputation by the time her bestselling historical novel, *Across the Bitter Sea*, was published in 1974. Acclaimed by the *Sunday Times* as 'a quite remarkable novel ... a novel of which Zola might have felt proud', this was followed by *Blood Relations* (1977), *Wild Geese* (1981) and *Citizen Burke* (1984). In 1982 she published *Inside Ireland*, a personal essay about the country, its people, places and history. Eilis Dillon was elected a Fellow of the Royal Society of Literature in 1979.

# EILÍS DILLON
## The Bitter Glass

POOLBEG

First published 1958 by
Faber and Faber Ltd., London

First paperback edition published 1981 by
Ward River Press, Dublin

This edition published 1987 by
Poolbeg Press Limited,
Swords, Co. Dublin, Ireland

ISBN 0 905169 96 4

Cover painting by Helen Pomphrey
Cover design by Steven Hope
Printed by The Guernsey Press Co. Ltd.,
Vale, Guernsey, Channel Islands.

Gaze no more in the bitter glass
The demons, with their subtle guile
Lift up before us when they pass,
Or only gaze a little while;
For there a fatal image grows
That the stormy night receives,
Roots half hidden under snows,
Broken boughs and blackened leaves.
For all things turn to barrenness
In the dim glass the demons hold,
The glass of outer weariness
Made when God slept in times of old.

\*     \*     \*

Thy tender eyes grow all unkind:
Gaze no more in the bitter glass.

W. B. YEATS

# CHAPTER I

Galway was like a different world. They all felt
it, from the moment when they first caught
sight of the sea and the train seemed suddenly
to become smaller as it rattled over the last little bridge
on its way into the station.

Standing at the window to look out, Ruth felt a huge
wave of peace wash over her, carrying away on its ebb
all the irritations and fears of the last weeks. She opened
the window wide so that the unusually hot summer air
flowed all around them. The others crowded behind
her, as if they had never before seen the little inlet of the
sea bordered with thatched cottages at the edge of the
town. Only Colman Andrews, world-weary with his
twenty-six years, did not move from his corner. Still he
smiled at them tolerantly, as if he could understand their
enthusiasm. Ruth turned and sent him a special look of
affection, hiding her disappointment at his coolness.
Then she said:

"Come and look, Colman. You can't see through
that frosted glass window."

Slowly and indolently he unfolded his long legs. As
he came across the rolling, swaying carriage, he stretched

9

himself consciously to his full magnificent height. His chin came up. His hooded brown eyes lifted slightly at the corners. When he looked at a thing intently, he had a way of turning his head as if to emphasize or display his Greek profile. He was doing it now. Ruth's elder brother, Pat, watching him, held his breath. He thought as he had sometimes thought before how he would like to spring on Colman and drag him down and rub his face on the ground. Pat thought of it like this because himself was small, and at twenty-one he was not likely to grow any more. He shut his eyes and waited for a second. Of course when he looked again, Colman was reaching for Ruth's hand and saying with his usual charm:

"Now we'll all forget Dublin completely. This is a holiday. No one may mention the war. Anyone who does will have to put sixpence into a jam-jar and we'll give it to the poor when we get home."

"I'm not likely to contribute much," said Nora, Pat's other sister, rather drily.

Colman looked down at her indulgently. Nora took no notice. She was seventeen. With the characteristic lack of resistance of her age, already she accepted Colman as one of the family, not to be given any special attention. Pat wished he could achieve this attitude. Still he found himself warming a little to Colman again, as he always did, and he was no longer impatient with the admiration in Ruth's eyes as she looked at him.

Pat had to admit that Colman had several good points. He paid proper attention to Ruth. He was handsome and clean-looking. He worked reasonably hard. He was pleasantly wealthy, for there was no one else to inherit the leather business that his father owned. Colman's only sister was married to a prosperous wine-merchant and was rather grand. But dismally Pat saw the obverse of each of these qualities which should have reassured him. Colman's managing ways might easily turn into bullying after his marriage to Ruth. They had only become engaged three weeks before, and already Pat thought he saw signs of Colman's tendency to inter-fere with Ruth's activities. Then Colman's good looks gave him more assurance than was good for him. A crooked nose, thought Pat, might save his soul for him. Even his industry had an air of selfishness about it. And here Pat came to the real source of his uneasiness.

The year was 1922. When this party had left it, Dublin was divided into two bitter armies, one battering the other in the ruins of the Four Courts, both armies tired and hysterical after the long struggle which had begun in 1916. Each side was willing to die for a principle. On neither side did the leaders care a fig for their lives. All of them had come to terms with death six years before. One side was disillusioned and bitter, but willing to build up a new state on the ruins of the old one. On the other side were the die-hards who preferred death to dishonour, and who were utterly incapable of taking an oath of allegiance to an English king. So throughout Ireland the Civil War blazed up, Republicans on one side, Free Staters on the other, and poor Mother Eire wringing her hands between the two of them.

Although he was not actively involved on either side, Pat found it impossible not to be concerned with these violent issues. But Colman seemed to take no interest. He had said once, rather apologetically, that before her death his mother had made him promise to keep out of politics. But seeing his detached attitude now, Pat was inclined to think that the promise had been made to himself.

As usual, when he came to this point, Pat began to blame himself for judging Colman so harshly. He knew that he was hating the idea of handing over his favourite sister to a stranger. If it had been Nora, he would not have felt like this. But Ruth was innocent and sweet and sensitive. He wondered how Brian felt about it, but it never occurred to Pat to ask him.

Brian was the youngest of the four MacAuleys. He was deep in conversation with Joe Thornton, the last member of the party. They had turned away from the window and were talking about Ansaldo engines. Joe Thornton was two years older than Pat, though they were at the same stage of the medical course at the university. He talked to the sixteen-year-old schoolboy Brian with the courtesy of a countryman and without the smallest hint of patronage.

The train slid to a tired stop in the echoing, empty station. Colman was the first on to the platform, helping Ruth down the steps. Nora jumped clear of his outstretched hand and was on her way down along the length of the train in a moment. Pat and Joe began to pile the hand-baggage on the platform. A middle-aged porter approached. His cap was pushed back off his steaming forehead. His black hair, spiked with the heat, stuck up in front of the peak. He looked the whole party over with lively interest and then said to Pat:

"Ye're going out to Derrylea for the summer? Where's the mammy and daddy?"

"Coming along in a day or two. We're going on the Clifden train at five o'clock."

"Then ye'll put all that stuff in the parcel office. There's more in the van, I suppose?"

"That's right."

Now Nora was coming towards the group, carrying one handle of a broad basket. The other handle was held without effort by a tall, slender girl with blue-black hair. The porter hurried forward to help them, but he stopped dead when he saw the contents of the basket.

"Blessed hour!" he said reverently, "Two of them! Who owns them, would you mind telling me?"

"Aunt Margaret—Mrs. Daly, that is," said Nora. "She's coming, too, in a few days' time."

The two babies in the basket grinned slowly at the porter as he admired them. Colman Andrews said, a little impatiently:

"Hadn't we better go at once, if we want to have tea before the train?"

He looked doubtfully at the babies and their nurse. Already angry that they had not travelled in the same carriage from Dublin, Nora said blackly:

"Sarah will come, too. I'll help her to carry the basket."

In a second, of course, Joe Thornton and Pat had the basket between them. Pat looked down at the babies and laughed with pure delight at the placid, miniature, identical heads, with their calm, bright eyes, accepting the world and everything in it without astonishment.

Joe leaned over with his free hand and stroked the little girl on the cheek. She grinned lopsidedly and rubbed her face against his finger like a cat.

Nora kept her place beside them as they came out of the station. Sarah walked easily beside Nora, with springy steps as if she were walking barefoot on a mountain-side. As was usual with her, her feet moved in the rhythm of the song that was running in her head. Sarah's home was in Derrylea, and she was happy to be going back there for the summer. Still her eyes were never quite free of an ancient, hereditary melancholy, like a Byzantine madonna.

They found Ruth and Colman waiting on the broad, limestone steps outside the station. Since there had been a market in the morning, the air was loud with the clanking of donkey-carts on their way home. Seven of them were passing the station just then. Each carried on one shaft a mountainous old woman in her best brown shawl, on the other shaft a man in heavy grey homespun trousers, a white báinín jacket and a flat black Spanish hat, and behind them on the cart the empty buttermilk keg and egg basket, next week's groceries and an armful of hay for the donkey. They moved in a sort of train, each donkey nibbling at the hay on the cart in front of him. The women shouted to each other about the price of calves and the gossip that they had picked up at the market. Suddenly the leading driver lashed at his donkey with his ash stick. The whole procession broke into a bouncing, clattering gallop and streamed off up the hill out of the town.

Colman led the way up the street to the square.

"Cattle-market," he said, sniffing the air in disgust.

Ruth gave a little shriek of laughter. He looked at her inquiringly.

"You have such a good palate," she said.

She had been about to explain that the over-strong smells of the market recalled far-off holidays more perfectly and instantly than anything else could ever do. But when she saw his completely blank and uncomprehending expression, she stopped. She told herself that it was not very nice for a young girl to have a nostalgic attachment for the smell of cattle-markets. She reflected that she must learn to cover up these coarse tendencies, lest they might peek out without warning after her marriage to Colman and disgrace him. But she felt, too, a painful sense of restriction, of which she was instantly ashamed.

"I love the smell of the cattle-market," said Nora heartily, coming up behind them. "It reminds me of when we first came for our holidays to Derrylea. Do you feel it too, Ruth?"

"A little," said Ruth hurriedly, glancing sideways at Colman.

Pat saw that look, and hated it.

Just off the square they crowded into a teashop. It was long and cool, and at this hour of the day quite empty. At the far end of the shop they sat at white marble tables with black wrought-iron feet. The chairs were covered in black leather. The dark-brown papered walls and darkly varnished woodwork were sombrely pleasant after the hot glare outside. They had tea and Bath buns.

"Heaven!" said Nora, biting the end off hers.

Sarah did not sit at the table with the others, but drank her tea at the counter, with the excuse that she had to supervise the heating of bottles of milk for the babies. She was shy with the strange young men. Also, Ruth since her engagement had moved into a new category and Sarah was not yet sure what to do about it. She found herself unable any longer to call Ruth by her first name. She dared not say Miss MacAuley, because Nora would have been on to this in a flash, with embarrassing outspokenness. So at present she was warding off from moment to moment the necessity for addressing Ruth by name at all.

Just as she received her bottles, two men came into the shop together. The older of the two saw Sarah at once, and leaving his friend buying bags of buns, he came along the length of the counter to speak to her. In spite of the heat, he was wearing a tweed cap with a peak, and a trench coat. Even while they shook hands, his eyes darted over her shoulder and found the group in the dimness at the back of the shop.

"Ye came safely enough?" he said anxiously. "Ye saw no trouble on the line?"

"Not a sign of it," said Sarah, in a low voice. "Were ye expecting it?"

"There's two bridges down now," said the man grimly. "They let your train through first. Ye'd best be getting on as quick as ye can. Were ye thinking of taking the five o'clock?"

Sarah nodded.

"Well, be sure ye don't miss it or ye might be spending the holidays in Galway."

"My mother is expecting to see me in to her this evening," said Sarah in alarm. "When were you out home last, Ned? Did you see her?"

"I saw her this morning, and she's fine," said Ned soothingly. "Wasn't it herself told me ye were coming today, and damn' glad I am to see ye got this far safe. There's no fear of ye if ye catch the five o'clock train."

The younger man had moved close enough to hear the last part of this.

"What are you saying to her, Ned?" he said, in an angry whisper. He laid a hand on Sarah's arm. "In two shakes I'd take her away with us. How do you know she won't tell the world what you're after saying to her?"

Sarah's eyes were fixed with fear. She made no attempt to shake the man's hand off. Ned said impatiently:

"Keep your shirt on, for the love of Mike. I didn't tell her anything. She's with the MacAuley youngsters. They're all going up to Derrylea on the five o'clock and I told her they shouldn't miss it. That's all. Look at them over there, as quiet and as harmless as a nest of field-mice."

"Who's the two strangers?" the other asked suspiciously, peering at the unconscious group around the tea-table.

"They're not strangers," said Ned. "The big fellow is Colman Andrews that's coming to Derrylea this last five years. And the little fellow is Master Thornton's son Joe, that you know since he was in petticoats."

"I didn't see him this while back," said the other, half-apologetically. "Well, she needn't go telling anything she heard." He glared threateningly at Sarah, but he took his hand off her arm. It was only then that he observed that she was holding a baby's bottle in each hand. "How many babies have ye at all?" he asked jokingly, as if he were trying to make amends for his roughness.

"Two," Sarah stammered. "Twins. They're in the basket, over."

"Ye'll be all right," said the man abruptly.

He marched out of the shop into the street. Ned said:

"You got a fright, Sarah, a-girl. Matt was made Commandant there after Easter and he's still kind of busy-like. But he's not bad behind it all. He's dead nuts on anyone that gives away information, and sure of course he's right."

Sarah leaned forward to whisper:

"Are ye going to blow up the Clifden line?"

"We are, God help us," said Ned. "We got wind of it that the Staters are going to bring men to Clifden. If they manage that, we'll be surrounded."

"The curse of God on yourselves and your war!" Sarah hissed with sudden venom.

"Ah, now, didn't he say ye'd be safe?" said Ned. "And sure, that means that no harm will be done until your train is gone over. Don't make me sorry I warned you."

"I won't," said Sarah. "I won't say a word."

Ned looked her over doubtfully. Then, with an impatient shake of his shoulders, he followed his Commandant out of the shop.

# CHAPTER II

When she was back with the others, Sarah did not speak of her conversation with the two men at the counter. Brian seemed to be the only one who had noticed them, and he was not given to asking questions. Nora took one of the bottles and said:

"Bags I to feed Paul."

"All right."

Sarah was secretly pleased, though she would give no sign of her preference for the little girl. Now, as she held the soft, warm, little body on her arm she felt comforted, as if she and the baby were protecting each other. It was not that she was still afraid. She was angry with that Commandant Matt for frightening her, but most of all she felt the heavy responsibility of the knowledge of their danger. Sarah had small respect for the efficiency of these amateur, trench-coated soldiers, though she had to admit that in past engagements they had never shown themselves wanting in courage. Vaguely she felt that they had no right to call themselves an army at all unless they marched into battle in shining uniforms, four abreast, on some huge, dim field long prepared for them by remote gods of war.

When the babies were fed, they bought éclairs at the

counter and came out again into the sunny street. They walked slowly towards Eyre Square. Already the heat of the day was less and a breeze from the sea was blowing the stench of the market away inland. Around the square, the grey limestone houses seemed to taper upwards in airy pyramids against the clear blue sky. Here and there, dejected-looking boys, dressed in identical homespun knickerbocker suits and caps, tended pens of forgotten, miserable calves. Hopelessly the boys watched the humming doorways of all the public-houses about. Each had a careless, cruel, forgetful father in there, pouring too much of the day's small profits in a long guilty stream of black porter down his throat. Each boy knew that in the dim evening he would be given a minute bag of bulls' eyes by way of compensation for neglect and as a bribe for a shut mouth. They bent their necks like the calves and dreamed of the coming times when they would be grown up and as wicked as their fathers were now.

"The donkeys and horses are taken away to a stable and fed," Pat remarked, "but the boys are left standing all day on the square. Why is that, Sarah?"

"I don't know, faith," said Sarah. "But the boys do be mad to come in to Galway. They'll have terrible boasting over the girls when they go home, telling about the fine times they had."

Half of the square was taken up with a tiny park, ringed with menacing black iron railings. Right by its entrance gate a row of side-cars was drawn up, horses and jarveys dozing comfortably. The foremost jarvey opened one eye and asked sleepily:

"Where would ye all be going?"

"To the station," said Pat.

The jarvey gave a little, happy laugh.

"Ye're no good to me, so," he said, and closed his eye again.

With one expert flick he knocked his battered black bowler hat forward on to his forehead. Then he dragged the skirts of his ancient frieze coat around him and seemed to fall instantly asleep. The horse blinked and proceeded with his plan of resting each foot in turn.

At the corner of the square a knowing-looking young man stood with one hand resting on the door of a long open car.

"A tanner a head to Salthill," he said hopefully. His accent was not the local one.

"I wish we had time," said Brian, in a low voice to Joe as they moved on.

"He won't make his fortune in Galway," said Joe drily.

The young man seemed to have come to the same conclusion. With an impatient movement he leaped over the shut door and drove noisily away.

Colman, suddenly hilarious, seized Ruth's arm and marched off briskly with her towards the station.

"Get a carriage for us!" Nora called after them.

Colman waved a hand and quickened his pace so that Ruth had to run to keep up with him. A long wisp of hair came loose from her honey-coloured bun and trailed down her back. She clutched at it once or twice and then abandoned it.

Joe and Pat put down the basket gently on the pavement and changed sides. The babies were asleep now, with that business-like expression of a healthy, hard-working baby. Watching them, the others all felt suddenly tired. Though they did not know it, Sarah's air of gloom had affected them. Also, Colman and Ruth, by their departure, seemed to have cut themselves off even more completely than they had done by their engagement.

"I wish we were in Derrylea now," said Nora, with a shiver.

Joe glanced at her quickly.

"We'll be there in two hours. That isn't bad."

Nora stopped dead.

"Couldn't we stay in Galway until tomorrow?" she said eagerly. "Sarah's Aunt Maggie will take in most of us."

Sarah nodded slowly. Her Aunt Maggie kept a big lodging-house near the docks.

"Which of us is going to tell Colman?" Pat asked without expression.

The hope that had fluttered Sarah's heart for a moment died down again. Nora said:

"Oh, bother Colman! I suppose he wouldn't like it."

Pat thought what a masterpiece of understatement this was. He chuckled as he envisaged Colman propped up stiffly in bed, while Sarah's Aunt Maggie sat on the foot until two o'clock in the morning, explaining beyond fear of obscurity exactly why she had no children. Aunt Maggie's memory was good, and the ancient words of her doctor had not been changed much with the years. She had never seen Colman, but Pat was sure that she would love him. He could imagine how she would throw up her hands and shriek that he was the finest man she had ever laid an eye on. Then she would walk all around him, and remark that the back of him was as good as the front, and test the stuff of his suit between her finger and thumb, and compliment him on his perspicacity in buying such fine strong shoes, and warn him always to use plenty of oil on his hair so that he would never go bald. She might even call in a neighbour or two and show him off to them. Colman would hate every moment of it. Savagely Pat wished that it could be brought about. He knew that Ruth would see Colman's impatience and he wanted to observe the effect of it on her.

Joe ended any prospect of further discussion by saying: "It's almost ten minutes to five. We'd better hurry." As they lifted the basket again he added: "It would be silly not to go on now."

When they reached the station they saw that Colman was guarding the doorway of an empty carriage. It was being assaulted by a short, fat woman, whose brown shawl had slipped down off her thin red hair and hung slackly on her shoulders. Her girth was oddly increased at one side by the fact that she was carrying an egg-basket on one arm, under her shawl. Standing behind Colman, Ruth was looking a little distressed, but Colman was laughing. As they approached they saw that the woman's face was red and damp with anger. Sarah recognized her, in consternation, as a neighbour of her own at home. She darted forward and spoke to her in Gaelic:

23

"Don't mind him, Cáit. There's no harm in him."

The woman whirled around and rattled out her grievance.

"First come first served, I told him, but he paid no heed to me. All day I'm in the market with my eggs and my chickens and the basket is full up this minute with tea and sugar and bread-soda and sweets for the children, and every kind of thing. As I came in the door there I thought to myself that in one–two minutes I'd be sitting back in the train like Lord Muck, with my boots off and the basket down on the floor beside me, and nothing to do all the way to Keel but to be thinking of all the messages I forgot to buy. And then this young blackguard here stands in my way and talks his grand language to me like the Pensions Officer, and won't let me get into the carriage." She gave a sudden little wail. "And now look at the bad manners of me, saying things like that about him in his hearing, so that anyone would think I was as ignorant as himself, God help me!"

"It's all right," said Sarah. "He doesn't understand Gaelic. But the others all do, of course."

Cáit had known Pat since he was a small boy. Still she was so flustered that she looked at him now as if he had been a stranger. He said quickly:

"There's room for us all. Give me the basket." He turned to Colman and said in English, trying to keep the anger out of his tone: "She's tired. Her sense of humour hasn't lasted through the heat of the day. You'd better help her up into that carriage as fast as you can."

Colman gave in at once, of course. Cáit's anger had evaporated, and now she had to be persuaded to climb into the carriage to which she had been laying siege only a few moments before. They got her settled in the best corner at last. Joe sat beside her and helped her to unlace her boots. His father had been the schoolmaster at Derrylea once, and Joe soon diverted her by telling her all the family news. She was overcome with admiration and delight when he told her that he was going to be a doctor.

"Though there's great sense in the old cures, too," she said earnestly.

By this time the others had all come into the carriage. The porter, oddly silent now, put in the last of the hand-baggage and jumped down on to the platform, banging the door loudly. Self-consciously, Sarah took the seat in front of Cáit, who now noticed the babies for the first time. She occupied herself thenceforward in instructing Sarah in a low voice on the care of babies, and in urging her to be very watchful of them so that they would be in good order when their parents would come. Sarah was well brought up. She listened politely and thanked Cáit for her advice.

At the other end of the carriage Nora was glaring at Colman.

"That was a mighty poor joke," she said. "Couldn't you even see that Ruth didn't like it?"

"Please, Nora!" said Ruth miserably. "Let's forget about it. It was all a mistake."

Nora snorted. Colman raised his eyebrows with an appearance of toleration, as if he hoped to make her feel small. He had already settled Ruth in the corner diagonally opposite to Cáit. As the train gave a preliminary shriek of pain and dragged itself out of the station, he turned his shoulder to the rest of the company and talked gently to Ruth, until she relaxed gradually. Pat stood up impatiently and leaned against the window to look at the passing scene.

The railway was built on an embankment here, so that it was high over the toy houses that encircled the potato market. The market was empty now, except for some children no bigger than birds, who ran and jumped around the weigh-bridge. For no reason that he could explain, Pat experienced a great emptiness as he watched their bird-like wheeling and circling. It made him feel like a mean, Oriental god. He turned down the corners of his mouth and closed his eyes until they were no more than slits. Then he relaxed hurriedly lest Nora might see, and know, as she often did, exactly what was in his mind.

They crossed the high, white, metal bridge over the River Corrib. After that they travelled along the river's edge, past pleasure-boats and swans and old yellow manor-houses. Then they left the river behind and came in sight of the mountains.

At Moycullen, eight miles out from Galway, the train stopped for ten minutes. Most of the women who got out here wore dark blue skirts instead of red. It was a subtle sign of their proximity to civilization. They wore black town stockings instead of homespun, and shoes instead of boots. They preferred plain hair-combs to the beautiful, high, tortoiseshell ones studded with diamanté stones, worn by the women from the more remote places. Even their shawls were darker: one or two of them had the new ugly black, instead of patterned varieties of brown. They carried a special kind of basket of their own, with a hinged lid.

"Every one of them has money in the bank," said Cáit in a low, awed tone to Sarah.

Outside the white station paling, these dignified creatures climbed into the carts that were waiting for them and were driven off by their husbands and sons. For long minutes the train sat drowsily in the evening sun, while a young ticket-checker climbed laboriously in and out of every door. He seemed to be filled with a kind of melancholy excitement. He punched their tickets savagely as if he were killing them one by one. Sarah wanted to ask him a question but she could not discover how to word it without revealing that she had been warned of their danger. The checker was a stranger to her. He seemed to make a point of not catching anyone's eye. When he had gone she began to say to herself a little rhymed prayer in Gaelic, that she had always known:

> "Oh Mary of Graces,
> Mother of the son of God,
> Keep us always
> On the right road.
> Save us all
> From every evil.
> Save us all
> Both soul and body."

Presently the train moved on, with doors heavily slammed in the dusty silence. Now the railway went through marshy country, crossing many tiny bridges over streams and little rushing rivers. Here and there little side roads, sometimes no more than tracks, crossed the line on their way to the farms at the foot of the mountains. Most of the farms were placed with nice precision on the dry belt between the wet mountain above and the wet bog below. The little houses and their garden walls were brilliantly white-washed. Nasturtiums and wallflowers and fat pink cabbage roses glowed strongly against the white walls. Children and sheep-dogs ran out to stare at the passing train. They had time to examine it closely, for it was the most leisurely train in the whole world. It was almost half-past six by the time it reached Keel, thirty miles from Galway, and came to a sighing stop.

# CHAPTER III

When they came out on to the platform Sarah stood very still. Only now did she understand how frightened she had been. She recognized it as the same feeling that she used to have at school when old Miss Gwynn would be bad-tempered, and her fierce eye, unnaturally round, would travel slowly along the rows of desks on the watch for the smallest hint of insubordination. Even now Sarah shivered as she remembered her. Miss Gwynn had died in the big 'flu four years ago. Sarah had danced with delight at the news of her death and had wished her in the next world a fine taste of what she had been accustomed to hand out in this. Then she had suffered from remorse and had told the curate about it in confession. He had made her pray for Miss Gwynn. She did as she was told, of course, but her heart was not in it.

From the moment of reaching the platform, Sarah had seen out of the corner of her eye that the three men who made up the entire staff of the station were gathered around the ticket-checker. The driver and fireman stood on the footplate of the engine to listen. No one took any notice of the passengers. Instantly Sarah knew what had happened but her feet would not take her towards them to make certain of it. The checker was gesturing grandly, fully enjoying his position of war correspondent. Now his voice floated along to them histrionically on the still air:

"Two spans of the bridge gone, I said, and he wants to know will there be a train tomorrow. Can a train fly? Can a train jump? Or maybe you'd like it to climb down into the River Corrib and paddle across and up the other side on to the track again?" He glared at the signalman who had asked the foolish question. "I'm telling you we're living in bad times, my boy. Two bridges down on the Dublin line and our own bridge swinging in mid-air like the hanging gardens of Babylon. And if I know anything about our God-fearing employers, we'll all be out of a job at the end of the week."

"Sure, they'll have to pay us, even if there's no trains," said the signalman hopefully.

The checker bent a solemn face towards him.

"Where are you from?" he asked portentously.

"From Clare Island," stammered the signalman, and added after a second's thought, "Sir."

"Back to Clare Island is where you'd best make up your mind to be going," said the checker. "You can signal the crows off the barley. You can signal the basking sharks out in the sea. But you'll see no train to signal on this line for the next six months, or I'm the Archbishop of Tuam!"

The signalman looked as if he were going to cry. Pat and Colman walked swiftly down along the platform. The others followed more slowly.

"Did you say there are bridges down?" Colman asked sharply.

The checker turned to him with a tolerant, pitying superior eye.

"That's right, sir," he said. "You might have heard them saying it in Galway. We all knew about the Dublin line being busted before we left Galway."

"That explains why that porter was so silent the second time," said Colman to Pat. "He must have known then." He flushed suddenly. "We'd have heard this if we hadn't been distracted by the red-haired Connemara woman."

The checker gazed knowingly from one of them to the other, and then with great interest over the rest of the party.

"When we got as far as Moycullen," he said, "we heard that the bridge behind us on this line was gone. They say 'tis to stop the Staters from sending soldiers to Clifden. It's the big white bridge over the Corrib, sir, just outside Galway."

"You should have told the passengers at Moycullen," said Colman, wanting to blame him for something.

"We didn't see no cause for distressing the passengers," said the checker with dignity. "We're scheduled to go to Clifden, and to Clifden we'll go unless we get a belt in the puss from a bomb between this and then. Come on, hero!" He slapped the Clare Island man on the shoulder. "This is your last chance to signal a train until the war is over. Now, Station-master, give the word and we'll be off into the night."

The station-master looked a little troubled. He was a thoughtful-looking thin man of about fifty.

"I suppose since ye didn't stop at Moycullen ye might as well go on," he said. "Ye have a few passengers for Clifden, anyhow."

"We have, and goods," said the checker firmly. "And if it's all the same to you, I don't want to spend the rest of the war in Keel."

The Connemara people seemed to accept quietly the news of the disruption of their line of communication with Galway. Only one woman moaned a little about her daughter who was in hospital there. With a hopeless air she allowed herself to be soothed and she left the station walking distractedly among her neighbours.

Sarah held Cáit back from following them, for she knew that there would be room for her on one of the sidecars.

"I wish we had stayed in Galway," said Nora, as they all helped to unload the luggage. "Now the others won't be able to come."

"They won't be able to come even as far as Galway," Joe pointed out.

"I hate it," said Nora savagely.

"What?" asked Joe.

"The primitive life——"

"Please don't grumble, Nora," said Ruth mildly. "We must make the best of it, that's all. Perhaps it won't be for long."

"And Derrylea is not so primitive," said Pat.

"It will be fun to be cut off from everywhere," said

Colman, with a kind of false heartiness. "Almost as good as being on an island in a storm."

Only Brian had nothing to say. He went to stand on the footplate of the engine with the driver and fireman until the train was ready to pull out. At the last moment he jumped clear. He waved to them once as the train drew away down the line. Then, without returning to the group standing by the baggage, he went out through the little station building on to the road. He came back a moment later accompanied by a short, wiry man and a boy of eighteen or so, obviously father and son. These immediately fell upon the smaller luggage and began to carry it outside to the two sidecars which were waiting.

"We just got here this minute," said the man apologetically. "We were delayed on the road over. I said to Bartleen, there's the train, and the decent people will be standing there waiting for us——"

"It's all right, Roddy," said Pat. "We're only here a moment. Did you hear that the big white bridge was blown up soon after we passed over it?"

"The dirty blackguards," said Roddy, in a tone of outrage. "They won't stop till they have the whole country killed. The Staters that did it, of course. 'Tis like what they'd do."

"The checker seemed to think that it was the Republicans," said Pat doubtfully.

"Did he now?" said Roddy softly. He pushed his old cap back on his forehead. "Good on them! Did you hear that, Bartleen? Ha! That'll give them Staters something to think about! That'll soften their cough, so it will!"

33

And he turned quickly and scuttled into the station, bursting into little happy chuckles as he went. Bartleen looked after him uncertainly as if he thought of following. He turned back, however, and began instead to load the sidecars with the baggage. The basket with the babies was hoisted up and placed behind the driver's back. Then Sarah climbed up on one side and Nora on the other, so that each could keep a hand on the basket. Pat and Joe took the other two seats. Ruth, Colman and Brian climbed on to the second sidecar. Bartleen helped Cáit, panting, up beside Brian. Then he climbed on to the box and arranged the baggage around his feet. Impatiently he glanced towards the station from which shrieks of excited laughter could be heard.

" 'Twould be as quick to go to America as to Derrylea," Sarah called out derisively to Bartleen. "What's keeping your da at all?"

Bartleen blushed with shame at being made to look so foolish before the strangers. In sudden rage, he plunged down off his perch and charged into the station. The horses swished the flies away with their tails. Dust settled all over everything. Even in the midst of his irritation at the delay, Pat's nose wrinkled like a rabbit's to the smell of leather and horses, and the dusty smell of the dandelion flowers that grew tall among the rank grass by the roadside.

Ten minutes passed.

"I'll fetch them out," said Nora with determination.

"I'm thinking she's the only one that could do it," said Sarah, turning detachedly to watch her go.

On the other sidecar Colman was exclaiming angrily. Ruth's hand rested on his sleeve to restrain him as he burst out:

"This is the limit! I'm going in to fetch them all out by the scruff——"

But just then Nora came marching out of the doorway of the little building followed by the two drivers. Roddy was looking sheepish, though he still gave off emanations of excitement. Bartleen was flushed with rage and humiliation.

"I'm sorry for delaying ye," said Roddy, as he climbed on to the box of his sidecar. "I was just telling the station-master that I'd be over with the cart tomorrow evening for the rest of the boxes. He's kind of excited, like, about his old railway bridge, you know, being blown up and all, and I had to give him very precise instructions before he took in what I was saying to him. Ah, well, I suppose it's a big day for him, and we mustn't be hard on him. Hup!" he roared to the quiet old horse.

Slowly they moved in procession out of the narrow lane, on to the long, bare, main road that looked as if it led everywhere and nowhere all at once. Away off before them the little group of women walking home moved in a cloud of dust. The horses' hooves and the metal-rimmed wheels of the sidecars ground heavily on the sandy road. The two drivers sat high and straight, with their feet braced against the footboards. The passengers were acutely uncomfortable, except for Sarah and Cáit, who had learned to ride on sidecars at an early age. The others kept their hold by a kind of surface tension. Presently the ribs of one side revolted with a long, piercing ache that seemed proof against all minor changes of position. For each of them, this pain became so important that they hardly saw the glorious red sunset drowsing over the long purple bog, nor the turning flash of wings as the horses' hooves disturbed flights of plover by the roadside.

Going downhill, Roddy flourished his whip and cracked it over his horse's back so that it broke into a lumbering trot. In the basket, the two babies' heads began to bounce up and down rhythmically on the pillows. Sarah shouted above the noise of the wheels:

"Easy on, there, Roddy! We'll be time enough!"

Roddy held the horse in for a while, but presently he forgot, and flourished his whip again, and sent the side-car swaying and rattling along. Sarah stood up and leaned across to seize the reins.

"What in the name of God is on you, Roddy?" she shouted. "Do you think it's coming from a wedding you are, driving like you'd be full of poiteen? Hold him in, I'm telling you, or you'll do harm."

"I'm sorry, Sarah, a-girl," said Roddy humbly. " 'Tis the excitement about the bridge, I suppose."

"God forgive you, yourself and your excitement," said Sarah sharply.

She sat quietly then, watching Roddy for signs that he was forgetting himself again. But he did not, though his mind was clearly on wars and explosions and the intoxicating pleasures of victory. Now and then he would give a little jerk, and his eye would light up. But in the moment of lifting his arm to make the horse join in the

36

fun, he would recover himself and dangle his whip dispiritedly.

In this way they moved along at a decent trot, crossing the main road from Galway to Clifden, and along the dusty winding road towards the sea. When the sun had set a little breeze sprang up. It carried a wet flavour of salt and seaweed. To Pat's ears it seemed to carry too the sound of the long, rolling Atlantic waves, whose hurrying tips spread in and in among remembered rocks and over stretches of hard, golden sand. Down by the edge of the sea, a darker patch of shadow was the wood around Derrylea House. It was a dream house, an unreal house that until now had ceased to exist from autumn till early summer every year, because it was empty of people then. But this year Pat found that his idea of it had changed. Some time during the winter he had discovered that the aching voids of childhood had filled up and that he could see the whole round world at last. It had pleased him immeasurably to find that the world was none the less astonishing and exciting for his new vision.

A quarter of a mile from the house they stopped to put Cáit down at her own door. Children peered out of the lamplit doorway and whispered excitedly to see her home so soon.

"I'm heartily thankful to you, sir," she said courteously to Colman, in careful English. "Good night to you all, and the blessings of God on you."

"Good night, Mrs. Conneeley," said Ruth gently. When they moved on again she said: "Please, let's not talk for the rest of the way. This last bit of the road is the best part of the holidays."

Colman made no reply. Watching her still, intent face in the dusk, his own wrinkled in anxiety to understand her. However, for all his huge size, the journey had tired him. He huddled himself in his seat and endured its discomfort without a groan until the two sidecars turned into the stable yard of the house, and pulled up at the back door.

# CHAPTER IV

An hour later, Ruth, Colman, Pat and Joe were sitting around an immense turf fire in the big, stone-floored drawing-room. After the tiresome journey it was a sheer pleasure not to move, not to feel wheels rolling, to be able to lean back in the old padded armchairs and breathe in the drowsy turf-smoke that swirled in little sneaking puffs from under the stone chimney-piece. Kate Faherty, the local woman who was their cook at Derrylea, had had ready a huge meal of eggs and potato-cakes and soda-bread. This, instead of reviving them, had made them more sleepy than ever.

Already Pat's experience of life had taught him that all important problems are better faced in the morning. Therefore he squirmed a little with irritation when Nora came into the room abruptly, saying in a tone that betrayed a small trace of satisfaction:

"There's only enough flour in the kitchen for another day or two. Kate says that Fahy's shop was expecting flour on the train from Galway today, but that it hasn't come."

"I'll scout around for some tomorrow," said Joe quickly.

"And Paul has a tooth!" said Nora triumphantly.

"Are you sure?" Ruth asked, glad of a more cheerful subject of conversation. "And what about Jane?"

"Of course I'm sure," said Nora. "He bit my finger with it. Jane is away behind him in every way. She hasn't a sign of a tooth. Sarah tried very hard to find one but she couldn't."

"What was your finger doing in Paul's mouth?" Colman asked, a little superciliously.

"Feeling for a tooth, of course, smarty," said Nora sharply. "And, Ruth, something will have to be done about the flies. They're everywhere, all over the kitchen table, and the walls, and the ceiling, on the bread, in the milk——"

"Stop it! You're disgusting!" Ruth sprang to her feet. Her eyes were full of angry tears. "I know you didn't want to come here. You're determined to spoil it for us all!"

She ran out of the room. Anyone else but Ruth would have slammed the door. She closed it sharply but without a sound. The turf ashes on the hearth lifted and whirled and settled again. Nora moved her shoulders helplessly and looked at the others. Colman started up in his chair as if to follow Ruth and then changed his mind. Pat said, avoiding Nora's eye:

"She should go to bed now, in any case."

The door was thrown open again and Brian came in, staggering under a double armful of struggling cats. He kicked the door shut with his heel and put the cats down. They ran about for a moment, like scraps of paper in the wind, before moving in little springs towards the fire.

There were five of them, a tortoiseshell mother and four variegated, stiff-tailed kittens almost full-grown. They were as neat and complete and individual as ballet dancers. Brian said quickly:

"What's the matter with Ruth?"

"She's gone to bed," said Pat shortly.

"I'll take Joanna up to her," said Brian, after a moment's pause. "Joanna is a comfort."

He captured the mother cat and carried her away. There was an uneasy silence when he had gone. Then Nora said:

"Pat, the flies really are very bad. I'm not just complaining, whatever Ruth may say."

"What does Sarah say about them?"

"We didn't talk about them, we just swished them away. Sarah is gone over to her mother's place now."

"We'll get after the flies in the morning," said Pat. "Don't worry about them."

But later, when he and Joe were going to bed in the big front room that they were sharing, Pat said suddenly:

"Joe, did Nora say that the flies were in the milk?"

"She certainly said that," said Joe, who always remembered what Nora said.

"Then we'll go down and write a message for Sarah, not to give that milk to the babies in the morning."

There were two old silver candle-sticks with snuffers, one beside each bed. They took them and went out on to the wide landing. Huge shadows stretched themselves tiredly all around them. Even at night it was a friendly house. A dim line of light showed under Col-

man's door, but Nora's and Ruth's were already black.
Brian slept in a small room at the end of a passage that
ran along by the side of the house. Sarah and the babies
had a room off this passage too.

They went into the drawing-room first, to get some
paper. Kate had covered the fire over with ashes so that
it looked like a tiny volcano. She had pulled back the
curtains too, and the two candle-flames, reflected in the
ink-black window-panes, glared in at them like a
dragon's eyes. In the silence they could hear the wash of
the sea below the house. Pat yawned widely as he wrote
the message at the table.

The kitchen was glowing with warmth from the
range. Like most of the ground-floor rooms, it was
flagged. Its long, narrow table and straw-bottomed
chairs surely dated from the time when the house was
built. Pat propped his piece of paper against a jug on the
table, and anchored it against draughts with a spoon.
Then he and Joe cut several slices of soda-bread at the
side table, buttered them thickly and bore them off upstairs again, piled high on a blue-flowered dinner-plate.

They sat silently but amicably munching on their beds
in the gloom. When they had finished and had got into
bed, Pat held the snuffer over his candle for a moment,
not wanting to make the world vanish. Then he pressed
it down over the flame, so slowly that the snuffer had
time to heat up and scorch his fingers. Joe's voice came
to him calmly out of the darkness:

"I think it was the way that Nora called Colman
'smarty' that upset Ruth, more than her talk about the

flies. Tomorrow I'll see if I can show her how to be more tactful. Funny how people who are engaged always want you to take them so seriously."

Pat did not answer. He knew that Joe did not expect it. A moment later he went on:

"Tomorrow we must organize things. We must see about food first. I'll go on the sidecar with Roddy to Keel, if you like, when he's going to fetch the luggage in the afternoon. I think I know where to get flour, all right. Are you asleep, Pat?"

"Almost. You're always a night planner. I like to put off my planning till the morning."

In the silence that followed, the sea seemed suddenly to become more insistent. Pat was not nearly asleep. Counting the waves as they crashed on to the beach became a monstrous bore, like counting the sections of railway line as the train passes over each joint. He listened for other sounds. Owls were hooting in the trees around the house. Every owl in that part of Connemara had to live in Derrylea wood, because there were no other trees. A bat squeaked sharply outside, so loud that he must have been just at the open window. There was a curlew crying too, and then a terrible, long wail, followed by the light, joyful, echoing bark of a fox. The bark of a fox is more like a laugh, Pat thought. And ducks laugh like a dreadful old man. He wished he could fall asleep, and immediately did.

Nora heard that bat, too. She hated bats. They got in your hair. They were simply covered with fleas. Her curtains were open so that she could see the dark grey of the night sky, full of fluttering shadows. She thought of

Dracula, waiting until you were asleep to nip in through the window and suck your blood. Dracula would do badly in Connemara, because all the windows would be shut tight except in the big house. She remembered reading that the best way of discovering whether your wife was a vampire was to look at her throat. If there were two little tooth marks, then she was. Suddenly she prickled all over with terror, and had to fumble for a match to light the candle, and get up and shut the window, and sit wrapped in the eiderdown, staring, waiting for goodness knows what to happen. If her mother had been here, Nora would have opened the door most cautiously and darted across the landing, whipping away the ends of her nightdress from the clutch of long, thin, black hands. She always saw the hands as black ones. Her mother's room would have been warm and real. Everything always came right there. Savagely, Nora wished for the sound of a tram, or the yellow of a street light through the window, or the late thump of heels on a pavement. Owls and ghosts and vampires always took possession of Derrylea at dark. At last she lay back, still wrapped in the eiderdown, and fell asleep leaving the candle lighting to keep the bogeys away.

Brian was fast asleep in his little, pitch-dark room whose window gave directly on to the deep green woods. He was dreaming of aeroplanes like birds, silent, with slowly-flapping, broad, white wings.

Ruth was lying very still, with one hand on Joanna's long, furry, sprawled stomach. Only her forefinger gently tickled the cat, moving rhythmically up and down, careful not to press too hard. She was thinking of

44

Colman, and of how everything would be all right if only they could get away from people. Her mother would have seen to that, if she had been able to come. Her father, too, in a more vague way, knew that she must be let alone just now. Her father liked Colman. He was the only one of them that did, Ruth saw bitterly. She knew nothing of family inhibitions, nor of the unconscious resentment against Colman as an interloper. All she saw was that what should have been a happy time was not happy at all. She began to plan long days of walks with Colman in quiet places, where one could sit down on grass and talk for hours together. Colman was all right when he was alone with her. During the night she wept in her sleep and disturbed Joanna dreadfully.

Colman had been reading in his armchair until quite late, until his candle had burned so low that it looked as if he would have to get into bed in the dark. He had timed things well, however. As he stretched himself deliberately between the sheets, the candle-flame grew tall and wild for a second and then was drowned abruptly in its own grease.

Colman always felt uneasy in strange surroundings. He forgot places easily, so that it was no help to him that he had spent several holidays in Derrylea before, sleeping in this very room. Still he knew that this strangeness was not the only reason why he was disturbed and uncomfortable. Now he set out carefully to analyse the causes of his discomfort. Experience had taught him that a vague malaise disappears when its composition is laid bare. First of all, there was the unwilling sense of responsibility, not only for Ruth, but for the rest of the

MacAuleys. He had never bargained to take charge of the whole family. Some premonition of their isolation had reached him before they left Dublin. It was when he had learned that the babies were to travel with the first party. He had got Ruth to try to change that, but she had not succeeded. Still, this could not be the cause of his uneasiness, because he knew now that Sarah was able to attend to the babies. And Kate when they arrived had made it clear that she was in charge of the house in Mrs. MacAuley's absence. Next Colman set out to think coldly of Ruth. But he could not. He dissolved at once into a bewildered piece of protoplasm, formless, without direction, almost without intelligence. His whole process of analysis broke up and floated away from him. Vaguely he tried to blame Ruth for his dissolution, but in a moment he shied away from this idea, ashamed. He squirmed with embarrassment as he remembered one after another of the unintentional stupidities that he had committed during the day. Then, with a sudden burst of anger he decided to blame the war for everything. He went to sleep thinking of Ruth, as he had done every night for six years.

# CHAPTER V

The early morning was pale, satiny blue. From the front door of the house, the ground sloped straight down to the sea. There was shingle first, still draped in trails of rotting sea-weed since the last storm at Easter. Then there was soft, gritty sand, difficult to walk on. After that came a huge horse-shoe of hard, pale-gold sand, bounded on one side by a long, black reef and on the other by a grassy cliff. A stream ran out at the cliff end, but it was easy to get across by the flat stepping-stones.

Ruth walked slowly as far as the stream. She did not cross it, because she could see that the grass on its far bank was still heavy with dew. Instead she turned down to the sea's edge, where small, thin waves left a silent, bubbling line on the shining sand. The islands were distantly clear. Every white-washed house on their shores showed up against their hard blue. All around her, the air carried the mixed scent of sea-weed and wild flowers, with a trace of turf-smoke even down here on the strand, that was the characteristic flavour of this place.

If her father had been here, he would have been plunging and splashing out there in the sea now. He believed in swimming before breakfast but he did not press his opinion on anyone else. Last year, Colman had gone with him once or twice, from politeness, and had had to crawl ashore, blue and shivering, within a few minutes.

As she turned back towards the house, Colman came out on to the broad steps. She could see him blinking and yawning in the sunshine. Then he came down the narrow gravel path to meet her. She noticed something peevish in his expression at once and asked anxiously:

"Did you sleep well? Was your room warm enough?"

"Yes, yes. All right, thank you. I was going to have breakfast when I saw you through the window. There's no one in the dining-room except Nora."

Ruth's heart began to beat heavily. His failure to respond when she had unselfconsciously leaned against his resisting shoulder had already humiliated and angered her. She glanced sideways at him, longing to drag out into the open the whole question of his relationship with Nora. But you don't start that sort of discussion before breakfast. An instinct prevented her, besides. She felt that her position was weakened by the fact that she herself had been so sharp with Nora last evening. Even in the few weeks since her engagement, she had begun to realize that Colman's protective instinct towards her was not without its drawbacks.

In the dining-room Nora was eating fried mackerel. Ruth noticed that she looked placid enough.

"The coffee is in our baggage," she said, "so it's tea this morning. It's going to be a most wonderful day."

"Yes, Colman and I might take sandwiches and walk over towards Cloghanbeg," said Ruth.

"Splendid idea," said Nora enthusiastically. "Then, when you come back, you'll find the luggage here and everything unpacked and Joe will have found out how we're going to manage until the bridge is mended. Much nicer for you to be out of it all."

"Exactly what do you mean by that?" Colman demanded with narrowed eyes.

"Oh, God!" said Nora, and fled out of the room, taking the last of her slice of bread with her.

Colman shrugged and helped himself and Ruth to mackerel. Ruth looked desperately from him to her plate. Then she said, in her low, soft voice, rigid now with control:

"Please don't take up everything that Nora says like that. She meant it quite kindly. There was nothing behind it. There never is with Nora. She's always doing things for me, like packing and unpacking my clothes. She's the sort that makes a slave of herself, in fact."

Colman waited for a moment before answering, as if to point out the futility of her tumbling apologies. Then he said in an ugly, hard tone:

"It doesn't sound like that to me. She makes no secret of her opinion of me."

Ruth found to her disgust that she was in tears again.

"Please try not to notice her," she was saying when Pat and Joe came into the room together.

There was no awkward silence. Joe saw to that.

"It's going to be perfect for a swim in an hour's time, with the tide coming in over that hot sand. Who's coming?"

"We thought of going towards Cloghanbeg for the

day," said Ruth, meticulously sorting fish-bones on her plate. "We don't know how long this hot spell is going to last."

"It's going to be the finest summer since 1884," said Pat wisely. "I've just been told so by Kate. She had it from her granddad. Or maybe it was 1883. Still, do go off for the day if you're not too tired. There's the remains of a column of I.R.A. about somewhere, Kate said, but they're not likely to come this way. If you see them, just go into the nearest house. They won't molest you."

"It's the same column that blew up the railway bridge," Joe explained. "It seems they got split up afterwards, and some of them have been caught by the Staters. This lot blew up the road bridge over the Keel River, late last night—too far away for us to hear the bang."

"That's the main road into Galway?" Colman asked.

"Yes. Fortunately it's at the far side of our baggage."

"We should never have left Dublin," said Colman, querulously unhelpful.

"Dublin was a great deal less peaceful than Derrylea, when I saw it last," said Pat drily. "Anyway, they say it will all be over by the end of the summer."

"Where did I hear that before?" said Joe sardonically.

"Let's not think about it," said Ruth, seeing the beginning of a long discussion. "I'll see Kate now and get some food. Can you be ready in ten minutes, Colman?"

Later, Pat and Joe went down to the beach to swim. Brian disappeared, after a late breakfast in the kitchen. Skulking upstairs, pretending to be busy unpacking and arranging her room, Nora waited until the house felt clean and empty before coming downstairs. Thus it was that she was the first to be told that the baby, Paul, was ill.

Sarah had the two cradles side by side out on the steps in the sun. They were closely covered with muslin. The air about them was loud with the humming of insects. Clouds of iridescent green and purple flies hung about the virginia creeper, darting in and out in well-regulated patterns of movement. House flies swarmed about the cradles, buzzing madly as if they were enraged at being excluded from them. Sarah slapped at them angrily.

"It's surely one of those fellows that's after making him sick," she said. "I never saw such a plague of them in all my born days. But I can't see how it could have happened. The milk was perfect. I found a note from the boys this morning about it, but they needn't have bothered. I had my own jug of milk last night, rightly boiled, and I filled the bottles out of that. You were with me yourself. I gave them a bottle each and put the rest away in the dairy for the night. I covered the bottles over well in there. Maybe someone moved the cloth— Nora, a-girl, what's the matter?"

Nora had turned away with a dreadful little gesture of her hand. A moment later she sprang across to twitch the muslin cover away from Paul's cradle. Immediately a fly darted in and landed on his forehead. He was a solid, round-headed baby. Just now he was asleep, with two clenched fists against his nose. He looked perfectly healthy except that the corner of his mouth that was visible was turned down, giving him an unpleasantly adult appearance. Still staring at him while Sarah brushed the fly away, Nora said:

"I fished a fly out of that milk-jug before you filled the bottles. I didn't know it mattered so much."

There was a pause. Then Sarah said briskly:

"Perhaps it won't matter. Maybe he'll be all right in the evening."

"Do you think he will?"

"I don't know. Jane seems perfect, though she had the same as Paul. Don't tell anyone about the fly. It's not anyone's business, as far as I can see."

"I won't say it."

Sarah took the muslin out of Nora's hand and adjusted it firmly in place again.

"We can do no more until we see how he is in the evening. Come away over to Hannah Frank with me. I told Kate I'd fetch the eggs for her."

They left Kate in charge of the babies and walked westwards along the bare road through the bog until they came to the first cottage. This was Hannah Frank's. A short, stony lane led up to the door. There were roses and wallflowers in bloom against the white-washed wall of the house. Great yellow patches on the roof showed where the thatch had been repaired. On the way there, Nora had begun to recover her spirits so that she was able to greet Hannah suitably when the time came.

Hannah was a widow, but whether it was her husband or her father who had been Frank, Nora had never discovered. She had reared a long family first with desperation and later, as they began to go to America and send home money, with a kind of religious resignation. She was a tall straight woman, so weather-beaten that there was no possible way of knowing what she had looked like when she was young. Her black hair was parted in the middle and dragged painfully down over her ears into a hard bun on the back of her neck. Never a hair dared stir from its appointed place. She walked in great plunging strides with a watchful eye to right and left as if she were in continual fear of being circumvented. When Nora was younger it had occurred to her more than once that she would not like to have Hannah for a mother.

Her youngest daughter was a pretty, mousy little creature of twelve, with curly chestnut hair. Her dress was heavy red woollen cloth with long full sleeves gathered into a narrow band at the wrists. Over this she wore a beautiful white cotton pinafore, high in the neck, with tiny sleeves like butterfly wings, all decorated with *broderie anglaise*. Her little brown feet were bare, set demurely side by side on the flags of the hearth. Her hands held each other still in her lap. She did not move from her place on the hob until her mother spoke sharply to her. Nora was embarrassed for her, and wished she had thought of bringing sweets. But she was glad, all the same, to be spared the worse embarrassment of Hannah's thanks.

Hannah put chairs to the fire for them. Then she built the fire up into a huge, unbearable inferno. It was all done out of politeness and the fear that she would fail in hospitality. Mesmerized, Nora watched the core of the fire spread until it possessed all but the outer layer of

53

turf. She began to move her chair back furtively an inch at a time. Hannah had settled into the hob for a gossip, insulated against the heat by her many red flannel petticoats.

"You're going to Mary Tommy's wedding on Tuesday?" She cocked an eye sideways at Sarah. "By the looks of things ye'll maybe have a christening the same day. Isn't she the bold thing to be having a wedding at all with the state she's in? Them young ones has no pride. Wouldn't you think she'd go away for a while, or anyways at all not to have a wedding?"

" 'Twill be a bit of sport," said Sarah, with an uneasy glance at Nora. "I do love a wedding."

" 'Twas the mother's idea to have it, thinking maybe the people couldn't count, or haven't an eye in their head." Hannah snorted righteously. "I'm telling you, if she was my daughter 'tisn't providing comfort I'd be. No, faith and soul 'tis not. She was always a great friend of yours, wasn't she? Maybe you could tell me what makes a bad woman out of a decent girl?"

"Mary is not a bad woman," said Sarah hotly. But she had to finish lamely enough: "I suppose they got tired of waiting. And sure, 'tisn't for us to judge them."

"True for you, Sarah a-girl," said Hannah, suddenly humble. " 'Tis easy to be talking about the other people's sins, when we don't feel like talking about our own. Tell me now, how are ye all above in the house? Isn't it a fright about the big white bridge? The curse of Cromwell on them that did it. May they never die till the house falls in on top of them. They say there's a bridge like that going into San Francisco harbour."

"We were just over it in time," Sarah began.

"Thanks and glory be to God. Wouldn't it be the divil painted if the train was blown up, too? And they tell me there's more roads and bridges blown up since last night. Sure, we thought we were finished with that class of thing when the Black and Tans went away. But ye're all safe and sound anyway. And ye have Mrs. Daly's two babies with ye, God bless them. Tell me now, are they fine children?"

"They are," said Sarah.

"Say 'God bless them,' Sarah a-girl," said Hannah urgently. "What kind of queer ways are you learning at all?"

"God bless them," said Sarah obediently.

"The little boy is sick today," said Nora, entering the conversation for the first time.

"What kind of sickness?"

"The green sickness," said Sarah shortly with a furious look at Nora.

"God have mercy on us!"

Hannah blessed herself. Her tone was hushed. It prickled Nora's scalp more than if she had shrieked. Sarah said impatiently:

"He's not bad with it."

" 'Tis a dangerous thing, then," said Hannah eagerly, "if it isn't watched. But sure, ye'll all mind him well and he'll be in powerful form when his mammy comes. When is she coming?"

" 'Twas to be tomorrow," said Sarah, "but now we don't know when it will be."

"Ah, well." Hannah sighed. "I'll get ye the eggs anyway."

She had a score of eggs ready in a basket, but she made them wait while she sent the child outside with a can to milk the goat. Goat's milk was a good cure for the green sickness, she said.

As they walked down the laneway to the road again, Sarah said reproachfully:

"What call did you have to go telling her about Paul? The likes of her haven't enough in their own misfortunes without enjoying the neighbour's as well."

"I thought she was very nice about it."

Having experienced the relief of telling someone, Nora had already begun to forget the nature of Hannah's reply.

" 'Twas kindly enough, I suppose," said Sarah grudgingly. "But I wouldn't have given her the satisfaction of it. Oh, 'tis only my own badness, I suppose. Mary Tommy was my great friend at school and I do hate to hear the way Hannah talks about her, and in front of you, too. She has no decency. And I wanted to bring you to the wedding whenever it would be and now you can't come with the way things are. 'Tis all spoiled now, so it is."

In her vexation she had departed from her intention of not discussing Mary Tommy's predicament with Nora and this made her even more angry.

Presently, however, the warmth of the sun and the light freshness of the air outside restored their good humour. It was impossible to be gloomy in weather like this. Nora began to be ravenously hungry, as she always was for the first few days of the holidays. The thought of food made her move a little faster. And she would be able to enjoy her lunch in the undemanding company of Joe and Pat. At this thought the vision of her next meeting with Colman began to make itself unpleasant, like a series of little repeated electric shocks. She thought what an ass she had been to rush out of the room like that. How often she had been warned of the danger of a violent reaction! But as usual, she told herself bitterly, she had to learn by experience. She wondered if Colman would ever forget the ugly little scene, in all the years when she would be irretrievably his sister-in-law. Nora could not imagine a time in which every single incident of her life would not stand out sharp and clear in her memory. She never forgot people nor their words. Now in attributing this capacity to Colman also, she did not know what a mistake it was to credit him with as remarkable a mind as her own.

So as they approached the house she twisted and squirmed as if with a physical pain. When they pushed open the wicket gate into the stable-yard, it was almost a welcome diversion to find it swarming with strange, armed men.

# CHAPTER VI

All movement stopped when the gate swung shut with a soft bang behind the two girls. Then, from the far side of the yard by the wide coach-house door, Brian came hurrying towards them. The men languidly watching his progress and his meeting with his sister, had an air of detached desperation. Brian pitched his voice low so that they would not hear.

"I brought them here. They have a man hurt in last night's explosion. I told them they could stay in the coach-house for a while. They've promised to do no harm."

"Where are Pat and Joe?"

"They're not back from the strand yet. I'm going down in a moment to explain to them."

As Brian had begun to speak, a short, broad-shouldered man had moved in beside him and was looking eagerly from one of them to the other almost as if they were speaking a foreign language. Above the half-inch stubble of beard, the skin of his face was tanned so dark that the whites of his eyes glittered like a negro's. His watchfully intelligent expression did not become him. A fundamentally kindly and humorous nature seemed to be trying to break through and to be continually thrust unwillingly downwards, so harshly as to make his last condition worse than if he had been naturally brutal. He was dressed in an old tweed jacket with many pockets and a pair of trousers of a different tweed, secured against his calves with greenish puttees. His once black boots were caked with mud, and there was dried mud on his battered soft hat. He carried a revolver in a holster and a leather bandolier under his jacket. The others were dressed in the same nondescript way, except that most of them wore peaked tweed caps with the peak worn to the back, and that some had gaiters instead of puttees. They were armed with Lee-Enfield rifles and Webley pistols. One little man had a Lewis gun beside him on the ground.

Now, as Nora watched, he folded himself down on the cobbles beside his gun and began to clean it with loving concentration. One by one the others turned away and taking oily pull-throughs out of their pockets, they followed the gunner's example.

"This is your sister, Brian?" said the Captain. "There's a great likeness between ye."

"I know you now," said Sarah suddenly. "Jim Horgan. You were the foreman above in the quarry on the Screeb road there, three years ago."

He laughed delightedly.

"And I didn't forget you either—Sarah—Sarah——" He stopped, troubled at this loss of memory.

"Lynch," she finished for him contemptuously. "What's bringing you in here, causing trouble to the people, and Mr. MacAuley not here at all to look after the place——"

"That's why we're here. Ye can say we forced our way in. No one will blame a crowd of young people."

"Go on!" said Sarah. "Some of them young lads you have there aren't even able to grow a whisker, and you may be sure they'll get more than blame if the Staters catch them."

He turned his back on Sarah and addressed Nora and Brian.

"Look, we don't want to force ourselves in where there's no goodwill. You don't have to side with us or with anyone. But one of our lads is wounded and we can't go dragging him from pillar to post. We all want a rest and a sleep. That more than anything. We'll be very quiet. We're not in much humour for singing. Just say we can stay out here in the yard for a day or two. That's all we're asking."

"I don't see why not," said Brian eagerly. "You know, Nora, it was I who brought them here. I met them crossing the bog, carrying a man on a stretcher."

"Of course they can stay," said Nora. "At least I don't mind. But there's Pat and Joe. And Ruth and Colman will be coming back in the evening."

"We'll talk to them when they come," said Horgan. He swung suddenly to look at Sarah through narrowed eyelids. "Would anyone lay information about us being here, I wonder?"

"I won't, anyhow," said Sarah sharply. "One thing we don't want is a battle in the back yard."

"True for you. What about the others?"

"You'll have to take your chance, young man," said Sarah sourly. "You're not at this game for the good of your health, I suppose."

She turned away to go in by the back door. Horgan waited to see that Nora and Brian began to walk around by the side of the house to go in by the front way. Then he followed Sarah across the yard and into the kitchen. He found her deep in talk with Kate who was in the act of dishing up midday dinner at the kitchen table. Both of them turned as he came in. His expression was enough to fill them with terror. Very slowly Sarah placed the egg-basket and the can of goat's milk on the table among the dishes. He came softly over to the table, walking on the balls of his feet, his arms hanging at an odd angle as if he hardly knew what to do with them.

"Listen to me, you Sarah," he began, so quietly that they strained forward to hear him, "I don't want to frighten those chisellers—the young fellow that showed us the way here, and his sister. That's why I went through the motions of asking their leave to stay here. We don't ask leave to stay. There's the lives of more than thirty men depending on me. They're going to be well looked after. We're not robbers, but we have to eat food same as ordinary people. We have to sleep, just like yourself. We have a sick man. You have two doctors staying here. We were told that by a man over Keel way. That's why we're out in daylight at all. Usually we move by night. I'm telling you this so that you'll see that we can't take any heed if people don't want us about the place. Do you understand that?"

After a sickly little pause, Sarah said hoarsely:

"I do. Sure you know well we mean you no harm. Is he hurted bad?"

"He can't walk anyway, and that's a damn nuisance. Are the doctors those men that the girl named—Pat and someone else?"

"Pat and Joe. But sure, they're not doctors at all, only going for doctors."

Fat Kate poked her head expertly in between them and looked eagerly from one face to the other as she said:

"But sure, isn't that better than not to have them knowing anything about doctoring? They can bandage handsome, for I saw Michael Peto's hand after them—handsome it was!"

"When do you expect them back?"

"Any minute now, to their dinner." Kate pulled out a straw-bottomed chair hospitably. "Put your bo-hind down on that, young man—excuse my language—and I'll put a fine plate of mate and cabbage before you, that will put the brains working in your head again like new. 'Tis hard to be clever when your belly is empty."

And she patted the straw seat invitingly.

The Captain gave a hard unfriendly look at the great dish of roast lamb whose agonizing vapour had been filling his nostrils with temptation since he had come into the kitchen.

"No, thanks," he said firmly. "I'll have a bite outside with the men. Can you give us a few buckets of spuds? We'll make a turf fire—there's turf in plenty out in the shed. I saw it and I coming in. We have a few bits of bacon with us. I'll send a man in for the spuds when they have the fire started. Thanks—thanks, all the same." He turned back to Sarah, as if he sensed that she had more authority than Kate. "Have you a bed to spare, anywhere in the house? You must have a bed, because the whole of your party hasn't arrived yet."

"There's a kind of folding bed up in the attic."

"That will do fine. Get that fixed up at once, and I'll get some of the lads to bring the stretcher in."

"He's like a blasht of wind," said Kate with respect, as he marched out of the kitchen into the yard.

They listened for a few seconds through the open door to his voice sharply giving instructions. Leaving Kate mournfully storing the meal in the oven to keep hot, Sarah went to do as she was told.

She found Nora standing helplessly in the middle of the hall.

"Brian is gone down to the strand to fetch Joe and Pat," she said. "What's going to happen now?"

"We're going to take in a lodger," said Sarah grimly. "I don't know what the master will say when he comes."

"If he were here he would take in a wounded man," said Nora.

"Sure, don't I know he would. But I wish to God they went some other where instead of here. Come on up with me till we fix the bed for him."

They brought clean sheets and blankets up to the top of the house. The attics were partitioned off from the rest of the house and approached through a narrow door at the foot of a flight of stairs. There were two rooms one of which was used as a boxroom. It contained several piles of old books and a doll's cot, as well as many elephantine leather trunks which no one would think of using, because of their weight. Nora had often spent a wet summer afternoon here, reading the 1870 edition of the *Encyclopaedia Britannica*, with the huge green volume propped against one of the trunks.

The other attic was kept clean and airy because there was a theory that it would turn in usefully as a bedroom some day in an emergency. Its walls were papered in a trailing pattern of blue flowers on a pale grey background. Hot dusty sunlight lay in great drifts on its bare floor. Heat seemed to pour through its sloping ceiling, too, from the burning hot slates of the roof. Around the open window hung the inevitable cloud of frantic flies.

They carried the bed in from the other attic and set it with its head against one wall. Sarah was silent while they made it up with the sheets and blankets. This was enough to get the house burned down around them, she was thinking. No one would believe that they had sheltered these men unwillingly. Her forehead wrinkled in hard, angry folds so that Nora thought it would be safer not to speak to her.

Almost before they had finished, they heard clumsy steps on the stairs. Piloted by Brian, two men of the column carried the stretcher. The man who lay upon it groaned as their awkward movements rolled him about. Trotting beside the stretcher came the little gunner, peering eagerly down at the patient and saying in a strange, alien accent:

"Keep yer pecker up, mitey. It'll all be over in two shikes."

Sarah hustled Nora out on to the landing while the

man was being transferred to the bed. Through the shut door his shriek came like a knife-cut.

"Go down and see how are the babies." With her hand on Nora's arm, Sarah glanced distractedly behind her. "I got no chance to look at them since we came in. And send the boys up the minute you see them."

She accompanied Nora as far as the door at the foot of the stairs, saying that she would wait in the attic until Pat and Joe would appear.

# CHAPTER VII

It was strange to be sitting around the dining-room table some time later eating Kate's colossal luncheon as they might do on any ordinary day. The patient in the attic had been bandaged adequately if not handsomely, and dosed with aspirin to ease the pain.

"He got it in the knee," said Pat, expertly carving the lamb. "I'd say there's a chip off the bone. He'll probably have a stiff knee for life after our efforts, but I suppose that's one better than having no knee at all."

"He made so much noise that I thought the two of you were amputating his leg," said Nora faintly.

She shivered as she remembered the screams that had reached her as she stood on the front steps. They had been muffled suddenly with the sharp closing of the attic window. The silent air had quivered with their reverberations long after they had ceased.

"Funny thing," said Joe. "He yelled his head off before we touched him, but he was perfectly still all the time we were hauling him about."

"Like the White Queen," said Brian calmly. "He had got all his screaming done first."

"That gunner is a queer little chap—the one they called 'Mighty'. A most unsuitable name."

"No, no. Mitey." Brian spelled the word. "He used to be a Connacht Ranger." He pronounced it 'Rynger'. "He's an Achill man, he told me. He says he acquired the accent once, for fun, and that now he finds he can't get rid of it."

"The Captain, Horgan, told me the Republicans are losing badly everywhere," said Joe. "Nearly half of this column got taken prisoner yesterday after blowing up the bridges. They think someone gave them away."

"Colman is going to hate finding them here," said Nora.

"He'll have to put up with it," said Pat shortly. "They'll probably move on in a day or two, in any case."

"Couldn't we try to get in to Galway on sidecars?" said Nora desperately. "We could leave the house to all these people. And there's Paul sick and wouldn't take his food and no one coming to help. It's all getting to be more than we can manage."

"Paul sick? That's the first I've heard of it."

"Sarah was going to tell you after dinner. She thinks it's the flies."

"Sarah is a bit of a fusser," said Pat kindly. "It's probably that tooth you were so proud of last night—or rather, the tooth next to it, that hasn't appeared yet."

"Do you think that's all? I've been terrified—we were at Hannah Frank's for eggs and she blessed herself when she heard that he had the green sickness." Nora laughed nervously. "I shouldn't have paid any attention to Hannah, of course. Sarah said not to. Hannah gave us goat's milk for Paul. She said it was a cure."

"Did she, indeed? Sometimes these cures are very good. We can try it, anyway. By the way, if Paul is even a little sick, it would be mad to try taking him in to Galway on a sidecar. How far is it, Joe?"

"Thirty-seven miles by the main road, but we couldn't go that way with the Keel bridge down. It would be a good fifteen miles more by the coast road."

"Oh, well, I see it just wouldn't work."

Nora was pleased that it was to this friendly company she had made her suggestion. This made her think of Colman again and of how he would have hated the long drive into Galway if they had decided to try it. As soon as the thought formed in her mind, she knew she was being unjust to Colman in erecting him as a monster of selfishness and contradiction. She did not like huge, handsome, god-like young men. She did not understand them. They made her uneasy. They made her feel conscious of her long hanging hair, her childish clothes, her damaged finger-nails. They looked too well satisfied with themselves. They glanced at her and away again, dismissing her at once as an unsuitable accompaniment to their own good looks. Nora was still young enough to retain a child's insight into people. To a child a hunched back, a scaly complexion, a twisted face means no more than that a person can easily be identified. A child sees beyond all barriers of good and bad looks, right into the soul, and finds kindness and strength or ill humour and self-absorption, on which he can easily base his affection or dislike. She was angry with herself for caring whether Colman liked her or not, for she felt instinctively that by this weakness she had lost some of the detachment and independence of childhood.

Joe never made her feel that things were too complicated to be solved. When he was there, everything was simple and utterly peaceful. She did not have to watch Joe's moods, as with burning anger she had seen Ruth watch Colman's. If she disagreed with Joe, she said so. Then he examined her reasons without heat and presented his own for discussion. Nora intended to marry Joe as soon as he would have finished his university course. More than once lately it had occurred to her that he might become ensnared before that time by a tall, slender, well-finished and assured young lady who would know all the things that Nora did not. But Joe was small and black-haired and he had a face like a dried-up chestnut. Nora guessed he would not be the proper prey for the kind of girl she had envisaged.

Joe glanced at Nora from time to time as they finished the meal almost in silence. He saw her expression change between anger and uneasiness, and finish with a kind of tranquil inner amusement which was one of the things he liked best about her. There was always something positive happening with Nora. Joe intended to marry Nora in a few years' time. Now it occurred to him that he should perhaps tell her about it soon, lest she be swept off her feet in the meantime by some tall, handsome, clean-limbed dead-head like Colman Andrews, to please whom he could see that Nora was breaking her heart. He did not really believe that Nora would find Colman's type attractive, but he knew that there were many types more attractive than his own. And you have to be careful with heiresses. He had lately seen a whole family of them, rather less rich and innocent than the MacAuleys, carried off one by one, by a small battalion of misunderstood artists each of whom was a transparent mountebank.

Just as they were leaving the dining-room Sarah came in to say that Kate was preparing an immense tray of food for the sick man in the attic.

"It don't look right to me," said Sarah, "but I can't say anything to her without her making out that it's mean I am. I know I didn't make him welcome, but her hospitality will put him into his grave, I'm thinking."

Joe went down to the kitchen at once to restrain Kate's enthusiasm. Brian disappeared in the direction of the stable-yard. Pat and Nora went out with Sarah to look at the babies. On the way, Pat forced upon himself an air of confidence which he did not in the least feel. Only in the last month or two had he seen a live patient. Now in his confused state, it seemed to him that those he had seen had all been huge arthritic carmen or downtrodden slum mothers escaping from their horrible homes into hospital, for a few weeks of peace. He had never seen a sick baby. That was going to be in the autumn.

Holding aside the muslin cover of the cradle, Sarah watched his face. He knew that she was desperately trying to estimate the amount of his knowledge. But as he looked down at the still little head, drained now of all colour and seeming already to have grown thinner in the cheeks, he could no longer play at being a doctor. His eyes, when he looked up into Sarah's face, were as frightened as hers. Fortunately Nora was bending over the other cradle. By the time she had come across to them, Pat was able to say:

"I don't think he looks too bad."

"I think he looks like a little old man," said Nora.

Her voice trembled a little, so that what was meant to be a sort of joke became a terrible truth. Pat said sharply:

"Nonsense. Don't say things like that, Nora."

Nora knew that she should not have said it. Still she seemed unable to prevent herself from going on:

"And Jane is getting to look just the same."

Instantly they were across at the second cradle.

"She looks the way Paul did this morning," said Sarah flatly.

"Sterilize everything," said Pat. "That's the most important thing. And try to keep the flies away. Boil the goat's milk and give it to Paul."

"I did," said Sarah. "It made him sick. Jane took hers, all right."

Pat cast about for some inspired idea of what should be done next but his mind remained quite vacant and stupid, as if the world of which he had experience had vanished and left him suspended in space. Then, with slow deadly force, the extent of their dilemma began to make itself known. As agonizingly as Nora, afraid in the dark last night, had longed for her mother, Pat did now. These babies were the only children of his aunt's late marriage. Their mother had hurried them down to Derrylea, terrified for their safety in Dublin—clean, hygienic Dublin, where the doctors were so numerous that they were scarcely able civilly to pass the time of day to each other. There was a doctor in Keel who was said to be a great man to pull a tooth, when he was sober.

Sarah said:

"I'll ask my mother what we should do. She doesn't believe in pishrogues and queer old cures. She'll maybe be able to tell us the right thing."

Immediately Pat felt relieved. Sarah's mother had been housekeeper to a parson in New York for five years. At the end of that time she had come back to Ireland to marry a poor farmer-fisherman, with whom she had struck this bargain before leaving home. She had brought back money and knowledge, both of which had dwindled with the years. Still Pat knew that she was almost the only woman in Derrylea who believed in the power of science.

He began to hustle Sarah off to consult with her mother at once. Then he changed his mind and decided to go himself. Then again he decided to send Nora and Joe; he himself would pay another visit to the injured man in the attic.

At this point Joe came back from the kitchen carrying a tray with a bowl of soup.

"I won," he said. "Kate thinks that every human illness can be cured by a fine square meal. She said we're to tell him how sorry we are that he can't have more, but that it's all for his good and he'll get plenty when he's a bit better."

"Kate is entirely devoted to food," said Pat.

Norah and Sarah looked uneasily from one of them to the other. Then their own frightened faces relaxed.

Each of them allowed herself a slightly embarrassed smile. Pat said:

"What's happening in the yard?"

"Rows of buckets of potatoes boiling on turf-fires, all very tasty. I think I smelt pig's feet. Kate certainly had a couple in the kitchen, that were not there before. I restrained her almost by force from putting one into the bowl of soup here, to fatten it up."

Before starting off with Nora, Joe had a long, silent look at Paul. Peering over his shoulder, Sarah said very softly:

"Maybe we'd be better to give him nothing at all?"

"You can't do that with a baby," said Joe. "All the same, just don't disturb him for the present. I think we should take him inside. The sunshine is probably annoying him. And there are less flies inside than out in this weather." So they carried the two cradles into a small, cool sitting-room at the back of the house, and left Sarah there with them, alone.

# CHAPTER VIII

Ruth and Colman had not walked far, after all, because of the heat. A mile or so along the little road that ran around the inner edge of Derrylea Bay, they had climbed into a high rocky field that mounted steadily until it ended in a cliff overhanging the sea. An outcropping rock provided shade from the sun in the hottest part of the day. The air was full of the peaceful sounds of summer. Larks sang wildly overhead, then paused suddenly and dropped to earth again. Ruth made Colman sit still so that one came quite close, walking through the short grass bobbing his little crested head. Around them sheep nibbled busily, pausing now and then to call deep-throatedly to their half-grown lambs.

All through the morning they watched the tide flow in over the black rocks, until the trailing orange-coloured weed floated and then was obliterated by the shining blue-grey water. At midday they ate brown soda-bread and hard-boiled eggs and then Ruth dozed for a while, her head on Colman's knee. When she awoke he had a tiny bouquet of orange trefoil for her, picked from the surrounding grass. Then they talked about the huge brick and granite house in Ballsbridge that was already being prepared for them. It was a Mac-Auley house which had most happily fallen vacant just in time for Ruth's father to make her a present of it. It had delicately moulded ceilings, and Adam chimney-pieces, and a white-panelled dining-room, and a kitchen and range of pantries that Ruth had peopled in imagination with terrifying servants. Fortunately, Colman seemed to know all about furniture, and the right colour for carpets and curtains, and about blue fading quickly in sunny rooms. These were all things in which Ruth knew she must now take an interest, but it was uphill work and it made yet another defect to be concealed from Colman.

Today she did rather well. She took a stand on the question of a Nelson dining-table and chairs that they had seen in Dublin a month ago. Ruth had liked them for being light and curly so that now she was able to make an almost passionate case for them. She was quite pleased when he agreed to write to the shop about them and she was even able to see in imagination how well they would look with the Crown Derby and Ironstone wedding-presents that had already begun to arrive.

But unfortunately Colman thought of wedding-presents, too, just then and this always made him stuffy. He asked her if she had written at once to thank the people who had sent them. She said:

"Yes, yes, of course."

But he would not let her go on to anything else until she had said exactly how soon after the arrival of each present she had sat down to write. He said it was very important, and that people always remembered and held it against you if you didn't write at once. He said that people would be watching from now on, to see if she were really fit to be the mistress of a big house. Ruth wriggled with embarrassment at this and tried to turn the conversation so that there would be less opportunity for him to preach, but it was no use. At last she said, quite sharply:

"I always acknowledge a present the moment it arrives. It's one of the few things I do care about."

Then, when he saw that she really was distressed, he changed the subject, but with a maddening air of having scored a useful point. Humbly Ruth smothered her irritation. Her intelligence told her that there must be long groping for complete understanding. Though she had known Colman for many years, sometimes it seemed as if their acquaintance had only begun with their engagement. She did not know which of them was at fault. She rather tended to blame herself for resenting Colman's liking for getting everything clear. She did not want everything clear. She preferred things to be a little mysterious. Above all, she disliked having her own personality dug over and explored and its rare flora labelled in a series of little boxes like prisons. Still she knew that it was wrong to think of marriage as a surrender of liberty. That was an old maid's point of view. All at once the thought came to her that it would have been a good thing if she had had to escape from something into marriage—from poverty, or cross parents, or dull uninteresting work. If she had not happened to be so fortunate in all these things, a sense of gratitude might now be carrying her through all her difficulties.

She glanced sideways at Colman and found him stealing an uneasy glance at her. Then they had to laugh and for the time being all their strains disappeared. They did not talk of wedding-presents again.

The tide had gone out when they got up to go home. Throughout the hot afternoon the rocks had come up one by one like basking seals. Yard after yard of yellow sand was left bare to dry in the sun. Ruth stood watching the sea's slow drifting rhythm and thought how wonderful it would be if they could spend the winter in Derrylea House.

A few weeks ago she would have said it at once, working out details of how they would live, quite sure that it would not be taken too seriously. But already she had learned that you must be careful about jokes, especially of the wishful-thinking kind. Colman said they made one feel discontented. Indeed Ruth thought it possible that they did have this effect on himself. Once when she had said that it would be a fine thing to spend every winter in Sicily, he had looked so frustrated that she had had to mention the volcanoes and earthquakes before his expression had become happy again. He simply could not see that the idea of spending winter in Sicily had no connection whatever with packing up and going there.

They did not go back by way of the road. Instead they went down to the shore by a steep path and walked along the curve of hard sand below the shingle. Presently Colman said:

"I hope Nora will have got over her temper by now."

Without changing the rate of her steps in the slightest Ruth said softly:

"That was not temper. Nora hates injustice more than anything."

"I don't think I was unjust to her. She didn't want us to go off and leave the work of settling in to her and to Joe and Pat. It was as plain as a pikestaff."

"You quite misunderstood her. She doesn't like to be misunderstood."

"Then she'd better get used to it. The world is full of injustice and misunderstanding. Children shouldn't be protected from these things."

In despair Ruth felt her self-control slip a little from her as she cried out:

"Nora is not a child. She's almost grown up. And why should she have to have injustice and misunderstanding inside her own house, if she's to meet so much of it outside?"

"For practice," said Colman calmly. "In any case, she's too familiar with me for her age. If she's going to be popping in and out of our house, she must learn not to talk to me like that."

Walking beside Ruth, using such a light, reasonable tone, Colman did not see that she was white with anger. When she did not reply at once he thought that she was considering his words.

"The trouble is that Nora may not pop in and out enough, if you don't take trouble to put her at her ease," she said quietly, as soon as she could speak.

"Heaven forbid!" said Colman acidly. "Nora at her

78

ease is too much for me. Besides, you won't be lonely," he went on kindly, seeing a problem as yet undiscussed. "There will be your mother to visit, and the house to look after, and lately I always leave the factory at half-past four. It makes the last hour easy for the men, if they know I'm not about the place."

He did not mention children, though he had thought of them, too. There were two big airy rooms on the third floor of the house. There would be a nurse, of course, not an old bully in white armour like their own Nanny Ryan. And not a Connemara girl who never knew her place, like Sarah. Something between the two would be best, someone older than Ruth, someone responsible.

At this, it seemed to Colman as if a dark curtain was lifted aside from a tiny window, giving him a glimpse in at his own complacent ego, sitting in a rather vulgar attitude with its feet crossed on the chimney-piece. He had experienced this before but it had never done him any good. He had always shied away from probing too deeply, lest his whole structure might crumble away into nothing. Once very dimly he had begun to suspect that he was no different from other men, except in the chance that he had inherited wealth. This thought had made him unhappy for the best part of a week, until he had created a defence as carefully as if he would have to put it before a court of law. A man had to look and act the part of a good businessman for the sake of his employees, for the sake of his country, of his family, of the other businessmen. He owed it to himself. Yes, he owed it to himself. In this way he had achieved consolation and had resolved never, never to let such thoughts trouble him again. From now on he would look to Ruth to keep him buoyed up, to give him assurance, to add to him the prestige that always goes with a devoted wife of good family. So now he quickly applied his cure and was soon back where he had started.

As for Ruth, when Colman took her arm to help her over the rocks at the end of the strand, she found herself completely unable any longer to resent his attitude to Nora. She told herself hurriedly that these disagreements are traditional and are usually solved without much difficulty by civilized people. Nora would be in Venice at school next year. By the time she would come home, everything would be different. Things were always changing. This was one of her mother's favourite maxims, that what seemed important today was likely to have become quite unimportant by next week. Ruth had a deep respect for her mother's philosophy.

So it was that they came up by the path from the strand arm in arm, and looking as if they had never been other than utterly happy in each other's company. Watching out from the window of her bedroom at the front of the house, Nora found herself filled, first with irritation and then with something that felt like jealousy. It was their look of self-sufficiency that had this effect on her, she supposed, for she knew that she was not really in the least bit jealous of them.

She stepped back from the window so that they could not see her. The other anxieties of the day had not by any means softened her recollections of her last encounter with Colman. She had told Joe all about it while they were walking over to Sarah's mother's place. He had agreed that it was unfortunate that there had been a scene.

"Engaged people are touchy," said Joe. "Just stay with me or with Pat and it will blow over. Try not to be in the same room alone with either of them. Discussion only makes these things worse, even friendly discussion."

In this way he had suggested the new idea of Ruth's siding with Colman against her.

When Joe and Nora had come back from visiting Mrs. Lynch, full of advice for the care of the babies, they had found the Folans's two empty sidecars waiting by the front door. The column's sentry had refused to allow Roddy and Bartleen to drive into the stable yard, but they had found their way in there through the kitchen in no time at all. Roddy was tremendously excited at meeting the men who had blown up half the country-side.

"That'll show them Staters!" he kept on repeating, marching lopsidedly up and down the yard, while Captain Horgan observed him without enthusiasm.

He paid no attention to Joe's attempts to get him to come away to Keel for the luggage until Horgan said casually:

"We could use a man like you, Folan, a good sound man that's not afraid of a fight."

Within a few minutes of that, Joe was leading him out through the house again, followed by the silent Bartleen. They had been gone for more than two hours now. Nora had stayed with Sarah for a while, but the sight of the now restless babies had been too much for her. Then she had searched everywhere for Pat, and had found him at last, lying on a rug in the garden, reading a medical book. Brian had disappeared, too, but there was nothing strange in that. She thought it rather callous of him to have gone off alone today. Until last year he had always been her companion at Derrylea. Then gradually he had seemed to find her company inadequate. Try as she would, she could not conceal from him her boredom with mechanical devices. Though she had always suspected that he would look for other company some day, still she felt deserted and ill-used when it happened. It was a pity that Ruth was so taken up with Colman just then, how taken up Nora had not guessed until their engagement. It was all very natural and to be expected, Nora thought savagely, but common sense is cold comfort when you find yourself all alone.

From the window she watched Pat close his book and get up to meet Ruth and Colman. A flock of seagulls screaming on the high tide below the house made it impossible to hear their voices. Nora turned away as Ruth began to mime the part of receiver of shocking news.

Then with a little rush she remembered Joe, and presently she was able to settle down in the long glow of the evening sun to wait for him to come back from Keel.

# CHAPTER IX

At five o'clock, Kate brought a pot of tea and several slices of currant bread and butter to Sarah, in the little sitting-room. Everything in this room had an air of subdued decadence. Still there was a strange restful charm about it, derived perhaps from its remoteness from the rest of the house. A huge chestnut tree grew close against the single narrow window, so that the light was always tinged with green. From outside, even after all the long, hot days, the mossy grass sent a drift of damp air in through the open window. There were three little armchairs, covered in old cretonne now faded almost white. The carpet had once had a pattern, but now it was like a dusty path marked with the claws of hens. Big splayed-out shadows of chestnut leaves mottled the walls. A small, cold, metal fireplace which had not known a fire for many years, seemed to accentuate the silent uselessness of the room.

Kate took no notice of atmospheres. She put her tray down on a chair and then lifted the chair easily across to place it beside Sarah.

"Start off on that now, a-girl," she said cheerfully. "I'm late with it, I know, but I'm heart-scalded with the men out in the yard, in on top of me every minute for this, that and the other."

She pulled the third chair over briskly and sat in it, with the tray between herself, and Sarah. Only as she was pouring the tea did she throw a glance over her shoulder at the two cradles in the corner.

"They're asleep at last. I heard them yowling all the afternoon. I wouldn't have your job for Ireland free."

Sarah pulled herself upright and smiled tolerantly at Kate.

"I don't mind it," she said, as she took the cup. "If they were in their health, I'd listen to them all day."

Kate hitched herself forward on her chair.

" 'Tis an awful thing to be responsible for someone else's children. I'd never take on that job. Never. What will you say to the mother if anything happens them?"

"What would happen them? Sure, there's no child that isn't sick some time of his life."

" 'Tis true for you. 'Tis, indeed." Kate sighed in an artificial, measuring way. "But they do say 'tis an unlucky year for babies. There's four of them has died in the green sickness this summer already, between here and Manister, God save the mark."

" 'Tis the flies," said Sarah sharply, in fright.

"Thanks be to God there's no flies in here," said Kate, throwing a calculating look about the room. "What did your mother say to do?"

"She said to give them eggs in water," said Sarah, "but I'd be afraid. They never ate an egg in their life. 'Twould only make them worse, I'm thinking."

"All the same, your mother is a fine knowledgeable woman and she gives good advice. Did she say anything else?"

"She said sugar and water would be good, too, and I'm going to try that now in a while."

"Isn't it a queer thing how the boys don't know anything about it, and they going for doctors with three years, nearly? 'T would be a good thing if they could take charge, because then you wouldn't be responsible."

"All I want is that they'll get better," said Sarah without expression.

Seeing that Sarah was not touching the bread and butter, Kate stretched out a slow hand and took a slice herself. As she bit off piece after piece, meditatively she watched Sarah put down her cup and cross the room to gaze down at the babies. Presently Sarah said, very quietly:

"Paul is changed a bit every time I look at him. I don't know is it better or worse he's getting."

"How do you know them from each other?" asked Kate, reaching for a second slice.

"Of course I know them."

With sudden passionate bitterness, Sarah wished that Kate would go away. Her complete lack of understanding was an offence. Her attitude towards the babies was clearly such that there could be no conversation about them and for Sarah, to talk of anything else would have been impossible. Her mind was so charged with this problem of their safety that there was not the smallest corner left for any other consideration.

Well schooled in the wary control that must exist between neighbours, she lifted her eyes slowly to look at Kate, who was now finishing the last slice of bread. Kate's foot was tapping to some imaginary cheerful rhythm. Her head was cocked on one side while she savoured the currants. She was a spinster and old enough to be Sarah's mother. One of her brothers was a judge in New York State and another was not quite the head of the Chicago police. Naturally enough, some of their wisdom had penetrated to Kate through the post, so that she had gradually set herself up as being in some un-specified way superior. She cooked and kept house for the MacAuleys in the summer-time with adequate efficiency, but she was always liable to leave dollars lying about, and to hold herself aloof from Mrs. MacAuley's impulsive charm. She never denied that Mrs. MacAuley was the kindest of neighbours and the willing adviser and helper of the whole district. But she made it plain that this patronage could never have anything to do with her. For Kate, advice and money came from Chicago and New York. Lately she had even begun to acquire a faint American accent, which sat rather oddly on her Connemara idiom and vocabulary. She lived alone in the nearest cottage to Derrylea House. She owned the finest dresser of delph in the whole parish, which was easy for her since she had no husband to break it.

Sarah never made the mistake of thinking that Kate was stupid. This was why she did not use the first excuse that occurred to her, to get Kate out of the room. With the present strained state of her nerves, she knew that she was liable to be untactful. So it was with immense relief that she heard hurried footsteps on the flagstones of the passage outside the door. A moment later Ruth and Pat were in the room.

Ruth was across by the cradles in a flash, with one arm around Sarah's shoulders.

"Oh, Sarah, I wish I'd known what was happening. I should have been here."

With a quick glance towards the open door to make sure that Colman was not outside, Sarah leaned a little against Ruth and said soothingly:

" 'Tis all right, a-girleen. I'm glad you had your day out."

Kate had got up slowly and was watching Ruth's face with a kind of impersonal curiosity. No one was taking any notice of her just then. Pat said to Sarah:

"Don't you think they have got worse?" He was deeply shocked at the change in their appearance.

"I don't know," said Sarah helplessly. "Paul is worse, I'm sure, and there's no news of the railway being fixed."

Kate gave a little hoot.

"Not for a month and more will it be fixed, Bartleen said. And the road bridge the other side of Keel is down so no one can come that way either."

Unbearably irritated as her voice rose higher and higher, Pat said sharply:

"Doctor Kenny lives this side of the Keel bridge, in any case. I'm going over there now to fetch him."

Sarah said, with an urgent hand on Pat's arm as if to hurry him off at once:

"Do, for the love of God. Sure, he might know something about it. There's Roddy and Bartleen will be back any minute from Keel and you can get one of them to turn around at once and take you straight back to the doctor's house."

Kate said loudly:

"I must go back to my kitchen or those men outside will eat us out of house and home."

As she swept out, Pat looked after her with a slightly surprised air, as if he had forgotten who she was. Then helpless terror seized him again as memories of the dissecting-room proved to him that children can die. Though he recognized the stupidity of it at once, he could not free himself of an urge to run, as one might from an imminent physical danger. Impatiently, he wished that Ruth and Sarah would not look at him so trustingly. The fact that Colman had not come in here with Ruth hurt him, too, not only for Ruth's sake but because he thought that himself might have derived some moral support from Colman's superior age and experience. Then immediately came the realization that Colman would find all this merely squalid and disgusting. And now Pat became anxious that Colman should be kept out of the room at all costs. He started to instruct Sarah about it, then recognized that he would have to see to it himself. He took Ruth's arm and guided her towards the door. There he turned, and stopped, shocked into immobility at the desolation in Sarah's face. So might the widow of an African chief gaze after the warriors who had placed her in the tomb with her dead husband, and who now turned away to pile up the imprisoning rocks at the cave's entrance. Even while pity wrenched at him, a deeper instinct warned him that any display of emotion now would be dangerous. Yet Sarah must somehow be released from this tomb-like room for a little while. His voice was steady and light as he said:

"Would you trust Ruth to stay here with them? I'd like you to come up to the attic with me."

She came, of course, though it was plain enough that she had never envisaged leaving the care of the babies to anyone. As they walked along the corridor to the hall, Pat was pleased to observe how her feet lost their heavy plodding tread and she seemed gradually to come to life again once she was out of that oppressive air.

At the end of the corridor she stopped.

"Don't put Nora in with the babies. She can't bear it. Ruth is steadier. She won't come to any harm."

"Nora?" said Pat. "Why?"

"It's Paul," said Sarah. "She's daft about him."

She stopped suddenly and leaned against the wall slackly. In the long pause that followed there was no need for words. There sat the thought between them like a little staring devil, every moment with eyes more sharp and stinging. Pat exorcised it boldly at last by saying:

"Do you think Paul is going to die?"

Tears streamed down Sarah's cheeks as she nodded. She rubbed her eyes absently with the heels of her hands. Pat said:

"Look, Sarah. Look at me. We can't help it. We don't know what to do."

"I'm not thinking that anyone will blame us," said Sarah. " 'Tis just that I do hate to see a person so sick, and not to be able to give them any comfort. 'Tis like the day long ago when the foreign sailorman was washed up by the tide and no one could understand his language and he couldn't make head nor tail of ours, and he died above there in Patcheen Phaddy's kitchen as lonesome as the day he was born."

Pat was struck dumb at this. As they went up the stairs to the attic in single file, he had time to discover that the revelation of her point of view had helped him to clarify his own. For him, Paul had never been merely a chattel, a responsibility. But neither had he been a real human person, resisting and perhaps resenting death with all the force of his little tired body.

At the attic door they paused. Pat said:

"Let's not look too glum, or this poor chap will think we're going to put him out on the side of the road."

"This morning I'd have done that very thing," said Sarah. "But I'd take in the devil himself now, if he came limping up to the door with a good story."

The attic was blazing hot. Pat went across at once to open the window, blaming himself for having forgotten to do this on his last visit. A feeble voice from the bed halted him with his hand on the sash.

"I'd rather have the window shut, sir, if it's all the same to you."

"But you'll roast in here," Pat protested.

" 'Tis better to roast than to chill," said the patient. "They do say the night air is very unhealthy."

"Where did you sleep last night?"

"We didn't sleep much last night, sir, except for an hour or two up against a rick of turf out on the bog. I didn't sleep at all myself because the knee was paining me."

"Where did you sleep the night before?" Pat asked patiently.

" 'Twas a big stable, sir," said the man. "On the Galway side of Keel. Why are you asking me questions? I'm not going to answer no questions."

"I was only thinking you've had a lot of night air lately," said Pat.

The man stirred restlessly in the little bed. Stubble had grown on his face during the day. It was a narrow face with a long, jutting jowl and long pointed nose. The eyes were brown, opaque and shining with an unnatural light, like bog pools with the sun on them. The hair was cut short but for a lock in front, meant to show under his cap. He looked as if his proper place was in a currach on a high, rolling sea. There he would have been master of his fate. Here he looked lost and helpless as many countrymen do in hospital.

Pat opened the window a little and came across to the bed, which Sarah had been tidying expertly.

"I'll come up and close that window before it gets dark," he promised.

While Pat felt his pulse the man said fearfully:

"If you left it open the leather bats would get in. I do hate leather bats. I saw them last night under the Keel bridge and they flying in and out as thick as bees. If one got into the room and I not able to move out of the bed, I'd die with the fright."

When they came out on to the landing again Sarah was shaking with laughter. Watching her, Pat smiled broadly, infected with her amusement. For a single moment he was happy, appreciating intensely the special value of Sarah.

"That's the hero that threw the bombs," she gasped as soon as they were away from the attic door. "The gunner told Kate that he was a great loss to them because he was the most daring man in the column." She giggled. "If the Staters only knew that all they have to do is let a bat after him, the war would be over in this part of the country in no time at all."

"I think it would take more than a bat to rout the Captain," said Pat. "We'll be making a great mistake if we underestimate him."

He found that he was uneasy at the idea of leaving Sarah to go to the doctor's house, lest she commit some indiscretion, not realizing her limitations as a prisoner. He knew that she would regard the judgment of Joe and Colman as being no better than her own. Very carefully he instructed her not to do anything but the most ordinary, everyday tasks without asking the Captain's permission. Then he found to his chagrin that himself was held up, at the moment of departure on the sidecar with Roddy, by a steadfast though apologetic sentry who insisted on consulting the Captain before he would let Pat go.

# CHAPTER X

"The doctor?" said Captain Horgan suspiciously. He had crossed the yard to be away from the men gathered in a drowsy group around the coach-house doorway, when the sentry came in with Pat. They stood by the wicket-gate that led out to the side avenue. The sentry went back to his patrol. In the hot silence they could hear the wheels of Roddy's side-car crunching the gravel around in front of the house, as the horse moved over to nibble at the sweet grassy verge. The Captain jerked his head in the direction of the sound.

"Is that the sidecar back from the station with the luggage?" Pat nodded. "Did Thornton come back with the driver?"

"Of course he did," said Pat impatiently. "We promised you that we wouldn't play any tricks."

Horgan raised an eyebrow at him.

"I had a man on a bicycle after him in any case," he said. "And of course the station staff are all on our side."

Pat thought of the worried station-master and the signalman from Clare Island, neither of whom had seemed a valuable ally, but he made no reply. Horgan said:

"There's no need to bring a doctor here. That man of ours is as strong as a horse. He'll be out of bed in a couple of days. Young fellows are always fussy."

"You certainly are a single-minded man," said Pat, stung into momentary rudeness. After a pause he said, very gently:

"It's not for your man that I want the doctor's advice. Unless he gets gangrene I think he'll be all right. But the babies are very ill, especially one of them, and we don't know enough to set about curing them."

"Aren't there plenty of women about? Surely they know what to do."

"My sisters certainly know nothing about it. And unless this is your first day in Connemara you must know that the women here are never surprised when a child dies."

As had happened to him before, the use of this word sent a little shock through him and left him with every nerve stretched. Horgan turned his head away.

"I hear the doctor in Keel is no great shakes," he said after a moment.

Pat waited. Then Horgan said:

"I'll have to send a man with you. I'm sorry I can't go with you myself. Here, Mitey!" The gunner looked up instantly, like a bird, and came trotting across the yard. "Go with Mr. MacAuley to the doctor's house in Keel. Nowhere else. Stay with him."

"O.K., Captain."

"Thank you," said Pat to Horgan, and turned to leave him.

But Horgan followed him right around to the sidecar and began to instruct Roddy about stopping only at the doctor's house. It was six o'clock by the time they moved off. Pat had an intolerable sensation of being held back, like a man trying to drag his feet free of mud. When Horgan held on to the tail of the sidecar to give Roddy a last warning, it was all Pat could do to refrain from knocking his hand away. Perhaps it was the vision of the slow pace at which the tired old horse would march off that restrained him.

Nora and Joe had come out to sit on the sunny steps and watch him go. Behind them in the doorway Colman appeared, obviously looking about for Ruth, who was still in the little room waiting for Sarah to come back. As the sidecar rounded the bend of the avenue, Pat gazing back towards the house saw Colman move down to talk to Joe, and realized that he should have explained to Colman what he was about. He had time only to see Nora stiffen unhappily, probably at some untactful remark of Colman's, before the whole group was out of sight.

Mitey sat with his knees drawn up almost to his chin, so that he looked like a grasshopper. His withered, peaked little face under an astonishingly flat black cap and his tiny, skinny, yellow hands added to the likeness. He leaned forward and smacked the horse's shiny hindquarters.

" 'E's no National winner," he said. " 'Ow old is 'e, Roddy?"

"Twenty-seven," said Roddy. "That's no age for a horse. He'll live to be forty, with luck."

95

"Luck for 'oo?" said Mitey derisively. "If you ask me, 'e's 'alf dead already."

And he smacked at the horse again so that it swished its tail angrily.

"You leave him alone," said Roddy heatedly, in his heavy drawl. "That's a good horse. He won every year for four years in the big race at Omey Strand, when he was younger. I'm telling you, there was a time when you couldn't be tickling him the way you're doing, or he'd kick the backside out of the car."

But from the sidelong looks that they threw at himself Pat knew that this was an elaborate game for his diversion. He smiled to please them, in answer to Mitey's wink, and immediately both of them relaxed.

Dust rose in a malignant cloud from the horse's hooves and from the wheels of the sidecar. Roddy on the box sat high above it, but the passengers had to bend their heads against it like Arabs in a Sahara dust-storm. The grass by the sides of the road was grey-white with dust, and the bogland stretching away on either hand had a dried-up, faded appearance after the long sunny days. Presently Pat found that the whirring sound of the wheels, punctuated with little jerks when they went over stones on the road, had emptied his head of all its thinking capacity. He tried to prod himself alive again but it was no use. At last he gave himself up to a state of semi-consciousness which was rather pleasant, though he hated himself for the ease with which he was able, in the midst of this miserable predicament, to withdraw into a little calm backwater.

The doctor's house was a dark-green patch in the

heathery bog. Its walls were so completely clothed in ivy that not an inch of their colour showed. The small mean windows of the upper storey were gradually filling in with ivy so that every year a little less of the dull, black pane showed in the middle. Ivy had grown over the chimneys and was crawling along the gutters, lifting the slates, choking the ventilators, smothering the whole house and the life in it with its dark tentacles. Low bushes, stunted by the salty winds that swept over that flat, empty place, grew close against the lower windows. A sandy lane, built high on a causeway of stones, led in to a rusty gate made of thin loops of iron.

Pat knew the house well, for he had passed it many times. Still because it was several miles away from Derrylea, he had never given more than a casual thought to its owner. Now he looked at the house in horror as they approached it, wondering what kind of a gnome or goblin would live in such a tangle of spidery vegetation. Roddy reflected his thought in a carefully detached remark:

"I'm afraid you'll find a bit of ivy growing on the doctor too, Patcheen."

He walked the horse as far as the little gate. There he jumped to the ground and turned the sidecar with scrupulous precision in the tiny space at the head of the lane, before allowing the passengers to get down.

The gate was immovable, embedded in weeds and grass. Mitey slid through a narrow gap in the wall beside it and advised Pat to do the same. He made no apology for accompanying him to the front door. It was clear from his expectant air as they stood on the mossy step, after Pat had hammered with the knocker, that he intended to take a great interest in whatever would follow.

Almost at once, they could hear feet dragging towards the doors, nails clanging on the flags, a sort of shuffle and then no more. A primitive fear began to drift over Pat, like a fog. In the peculiarly empty silence that followed, his distressed mind even envisaged, crouching behind the cracked panels, some subhuman monster with ivy twined through its hair. Tired of the delay, he reached out suddenly and hammered with the knocker again. A bolt was drawn and the door swung easily inwards.

A small man stood there, looking from one of them to the other with a mild. inquiring eye. He was dressed in a knicker-bocker suit of dust-coloured herring-bone tweed, thick grey stockings and a dreadful old pair of brown, nailed boots that looked as if they had not been polished for years. It seemed to Pat as if the wrong head had become attached by mistake to this shapeless body. The small, fine head, with long silvery hair curling delicately over the rough tweed collar, would have been worth a fortune to a dandified city doctor in a tail coat and embroidered waistcoat. So would the blank, enigmatic expression of a man who guards tremendous secrets, and who must constantly commune with himself on the question of whether or not to reveal them. This air of mysterious knowledge was enhanced by rimless spectacles on slender gold wire ear-pieces. Though his clothes were those of a man who spends all his time out of doors, the skin of his face was pale and dull above a neatly pointed, silver beard. Pat said:

"Dr. Kenny?"

"Yes, yes, yes, I am Dr. Kenny. What do you want?"

His voice was querulous and a little husky as if from lack of use. Its intonation and the precise, simple words that he used had a vaguely archaic air. Pat found himself responding with the kind of patient lucidity that one would use to a small child.

"I want you to come to Derrylea House with me, now."

"No, no. I'm a sick man myself. Go away."

As he began to shut the door, Mitey slipped forward like an eel and dodged under his arm into the hall. The doctor dropped his hand from the door and beat at him feebly.

"Get out of my house. Who is this person?"

"I'm 'is friend," said Mitey, jerking a thumb towards Pat. " 'E wants to talk to you. Come on, be a sport!"

He gestured to Pat to step into the hall. Pat did so and saw, just before Mitey pushed the door shut, how Roddy on the sidecar was watching them with his eyes popping in astonishment.

"Now, mitey," said Mitey genially to Kenny, "show us into the parlour, do."

"I will not, you have no rights here. Be off with you!"

"This w'y, is it?"

Mitey, undisturbed, moved towards a door to the right of the hall. The only light in the hall came through an oblong pane of glass over the front door so that it was difficult to see the doctor's face. He darted forward to reach the door first and hold it against the little gunner. Pat stood by helplessly while they battled for possession of the handle. He could hear Mitey breathing raspingly.

The doctor fought silently but with a disproportionate air of desperation as if he were defending his life. After a full minute of this, Mitey slowly lifted Kenny's wrist away with one hand. With the other hand he opened the door.

"Come in and sit down, there's a good chap," he said in the conciliating tone of a victor.

He laid his hand on Kenny's now unresisting shoulder and guided him into the room. As he placed him tenderly on the dusty horsehair sofa that stood against one wall, he said in a tone of smug encouragement:

"There, now, ain't that nice? And your glasses still 'ere, safe and sound."

Still in a half-daze from the whole extraordinary performance, Pat shut the door and stood with his back to it.

" 'E'll be good now," said Mitey. "You can come and sit down, and Doctor Kenny will give us the benefit of 'is scientific knowledge."

# CHAPTER XI

The dismal gloom of the parlour was no surprise. It was perfectly in accord with the impression that they had received of the rest of the house. Horsehair and red plush chairs clustered in disorder in the middle of the floor. Broken-legged mahogany tables skulked in the corners, thick with the damp, scaly dust of years. In spite of the preliminary struggle, something had scuttled agitatedly in there, when they came into the room. There was a fireplace of old yellow tiles, appropriately decorated with ivy-leaves and surmounted by an overmantel in a terrifying state of decay. Ragged green curtains on the single window served to reduce even further the dim green light that filtered through the clustering ivy-leaves outside. There was a carpet of uncertain pattern, bald with age. Under it the boards felt soft and rotten to the feet.

Pat crossed cautiously to the most sound-looking chair and sat in it. Immediately one of its back legs penetrated through the carpet and the floor, almost pitching him backwards. He stood up angrily, feeling like the victim of some stupid practical joke. He wanted to attack the doctor, to shout at him, to lift him up by the collar and shake him senseless. But the doctor sat like a stone, exactly where Mitey had placed him. His hands hung down between his knees, almost touching the floor. Over his bent head Pat looked at Mitey in despair. The gunner lifted his shoulders high and wagged his little head. He sat down beside Kenny and slapped him lightly on the back.

"Wike up, old cock!" he said genially. "We've come a long w'y to see you."

"Don't do that," said Kenny pettishly. "I told you I'm a sick man."

But he straightened his back and placed his hands on his knees as if to prevent himself from falling forward again. He looked at Pat with vacant eyes, apparently devoid of all understanding. Pat began to talk to him sharply, urgently, trying to force a way into that dim brain by the strength of his own personality. At first it seemed as if Kenny were following the story with some intelligence. Then his eyelids drooped for a second. When he opened his eyes again they were staring. He said in a terrified whisper, like a man talking to a ghost:

"You must go out of the room, for a minute. Only a minute. You can come in again."

Mitey shook his head.

"No, no, mitey, we're not going to leave you. Pull yerself together and pay attention to the gentleman."

"Please go. Please go out."

His voice shook with excitement, and a little wailing note had come into it. His hands began to twitch and jerk and clutch, in a kind of purposeless agitation. He looked down at them as if he were not their owner, as if he were merely observing their antics. Then he drew in a shuddering breath and held himself in control for long enough to say:

"You're a medical student? You said you're a medical student?"

"Yes, yes," said Pat eagerly, pleased at the first sign that his words had been understood.

"Then get him out of here." He poked at Mitey, who was still sitting beside him. "Get him out, I say. Get him out."

He spoke in a high, light monotone which was more penetrating than a shout. Tears filled his myopic blue eyes and drifted down into his beard. Pat felt his skin crawl with disgust. To his eyes by contrast with the doctor, Mitey had ceased now to be an oddity. His intelligence and comprehension rendered quite unimportant his physical smallness and peculiarity, and the tricks to which he resorted to bring himself up to the stature of ordinary men. All these, even the strange accent, fell away from him now, at the sight of Pat's despair.

"I think I know what's wrong," he said in a low voice. "I'll go outside into the hall and give him a chance, the poor bastard. No tricks, now!"

"No," said Pat, not understanding in the least what Mitey was talking about.

Kenny seemed to come to himself a little when Mitey stood up. A cunning look came into his eyes, slanting them meanly. Pat was thankful that he had stopped weeping, but for all that he looked no more attractive now. Eagerly Kenny watched every step that the little man took on his way to the door. When it rattled shut he still sat watching it for a moment, with his head cocked on one side. Then he lifted himself slowly to his feet and walked awkwardly across the room, with the careful gait of an old turkey-cock. He stretched out a slow hand, tense and rigid with controlled anticipation, and opened, with one long, clean movement, a drawer in one of the tables that crowded in a jumble beside the fireplace. Fascinated, Pat watched that expressive hand, how it gave a little happy skip on the rim of the table, and hovered lovingly for a moment over the contents of the drawer, and flew up into the air in a transport of pleasure before plunging in to withdraw a little metal box.

Now Kenny was panting and chuckling to himself. He brought the box to the sofa and sat down with great care and with a kind of dancing shuffle of the feet, in the exact place where he had been before. He wept a little again when his trembling fingers would not open the box quickly enough. At last he succeeded, and held the little syringe it contained cradled in his palm as Pat had often held a frightened, fluttering bird.

Now Kenny's face became solemn and concentrated. He filled the syringe from a tiny bottle which he took from his pocket. Each little movement showed the delicate precision of long practice. His tongue only betrayed his excitement, slipping out quickly to wet his lips. He pushed back the sleeve of his coat and inserted the needle in the skin, which was speckled with the marks of former injections. Not a tremor shook his hand now as he pressed the plunger down through the little cylinder. Clearly the prospect of relief had already made him feel the happiness that the drug could not yet have brought him. It occurred to Pat now that Kenny had deliberately sat in the place where he had suffered his recent agony so as to intensify the pleasure of this relief.

When he had made certain that the last drop had been emptied from it, Kenny withdrew the syringe and looked up at Pat. His eyes were wide open now and full of a kind of surprise, like a man looking at a beautiful view. For all his revulsion at the spectacle that he·had just witnessed, Pat could not help feeling some measure of respect for the contents of the little bottle, which had achieved the impossible in turning Kenny into a human being again. In fact, he looked so normal now that Pat was embarrassed for what to say to him. Kenny was not in the least disturbed.

"I knew just before I opened the door to you that I needed a shot," he said. "If you hadn't made such a row with the knocker I'd have gone back and had it, and you mightn't have had to see my little performance. Don't look so shocked." His tone was patronizing. "If you can't put up with an occasional contretemps like that, you'd better give up medicine now and learn to be a typist. Though I hear that there are shocks in that trade, too."

Pat made no reply to this. After a moment he said:

"Where do you get it?"

"Morphine? Oh, that's easy. You'll be able to get it, too, when you're qualified." He laughed at Pat's reaction against this teasing. Then he went on:

"You'll have to tell me your story again, I'm afraid. I only remember something about babies having gastro-enteritis."

A tidal wave of anger mounted in Pat's brain again at Kenny's flippant tone. Then every emotion seemed to trickle out of him, so that he felt as if he were bleeding to death. Though he did not know it, this was anger too, of the kind that would use its last despairing, feeble effort to kill. Once more he began to tell Kenny the story of the isolated house and the sick children cut off from their parents by the shattered bridges. He abandoned quickly the idea of an emotional appeal when he noticed Kenny's sceptical expression. He told him then about the plague of flies, and talked of symptoms, and tried to pretend that his own attitude was impersonal and scientific. He even managed a dreadful little man-to-man laugh at Sarah's mother's cure of eggs in water. But he had to finish by admitting that he had no idea of what should be done, and by asking the doctor to come over to Derrylea on Roddy's sidecar and take charge of the situation himself.

Mitey had slipped back into the room while Pat was talking. This time he sat cautiously on one of the chairs in the middle of the room, cocking a knowing eyebrow at Kenny. Pat watched Kenny too, as eagerly as if the first words that would drop from that mean weaselly mouth would save them all from disaster. The doctor said:

"Did you give them barley-water?"

Patiently Pat explained that they had not thought of this remedy, and that even if they had, they did not have the materials to make it.

"It's not a remedy," said Kenny pettishly. "Don't you know anything at all? It's just that you must feed them or they'll die of starvation. And you may laugh at Mrs. Lynch's cure, young man, but her advice is to be found in the text-books too."

So far from being offended at the doctor's tone, as he felt he was intended to be, Pat was overjoyed at a sign of his interest. This was what made him forget all discretion and rush on to say:

"And I have a member of a flying column of I.R.A. in the attic with a broken knee-bone. You must look at him too. I and Joe Thornton did what we could for him, but I didn't like the look of him when I saw him last. He was a bit flushed and blotchy——"

He stopped, appalled at the expression of concentrated venom on the doctor's face.

"Flushed and blotchy, was he?" said Kenny softly. "You probably have typhoid in the house. That's probably what your precious babies have too. Typhoid. This God-forsaken place is rotten with it." He looked quickly around the room, as if it were a trap from which he must escape. "When you're gone I'll close up this room. I won't come in here again. You probably have it yourself—both of you may have it. And in case you don't manage to infect me with typhoid, you'll at least mix me up with your flying column, as you call it. I'll have nothing to do with your flying columns. I was never mixed up in politics——"

Mitey interrupted sharply:

"There's nothing to be afraid of. No one minds where a doctor goes."

"Don't they? A fat lot of comfort that will be to me if I get a bullet in the belly. I'll have nothing to do with it."

107

Pat stood up slowly. His hands were stiff. His legs seemed to move of themselves, stiff-jointedly. With his mind quite blank, he saw himself walk around to the back of the chair on which he had been sitting. Those senseless hands stretched themselves out and wrapped their hard fingers around the chair back. They lifted the chair in one terrible sweeping movement, high into the air, smashing the dry bowl of the swinging paraffin lamp so that tinkling glass flew like hail into every corner of the room. The sound seemed to set off a detonator inside Pat's head. He heard his own throat emit a sob of pure rage. He brought the chair down with all his force on the doctor's head. Then he hurled himself after it and began to pummel and hammer at Kenny with his fists. He wept because his blows were not powerful enough to batter out that miserable life and thus ensure that the doctor need never again be afraid of typhoid germs.

# CHAPTER XII

It was Mitey who managed to put an end to it. He was pulling at Pat's coat-tails and bleating like a goat. Through the fog in his brain, Pat heard the little helpless sound and it amused him. Then he had to stop beating at Kenny, and step backwards, panting and feeling a very little ashamed.

" 'Ave you gone batty, too?" said Mitey angrily, wiping his wet forehead with his sleeve.

His cap was pushed right back on his head so that the peak pointed to the ceiling, and still no hair showed. Pat regretted that it had not fallen off altogether, for he would have liked to see whether Mitey owned any hair at all. The little man said:

"Were you trying to kill him?"

"Yes," said Pat.

There was a pause. Then Mitey said in a different tone:

"You're a little fighting-cock, like myself." He sighed, and returned his cap to its normal position. "If we were the full size, we'd be a dangerous pair. Look at 'is nibs."

They stood side by side and surveyed the doctor. His

head was framed between the seat of the chair and its rails, so that it had protected him like a helmet from Pat's fists. His glasses had fallen off and lay, unbroken, on the floor. Blood flowed slowly from several cuts on his forehead. He was crouched on the sofa with his knees drawn up, as if he had tried to shrink through the wall to safety. Pat was reminded of a cat cornered by dogs. Again he felt ashamed, but more than that he was astonished at the way in which the little demon that had lived silently inside him all his life had broken loose at last.

He lifted the chair tenderly off Kenny's head and placed it upright on the ground. One of its legs was broken now, so that it tilted backwards slowly and fell. Neither of them touched it, though Mitey was picking up pieces of broken glass and making a little pile of them in the hearth. Pat turned Kenny around and placed his feet on the ground one beside the other. He looked at him helplessly, not knowing what to say to him. Everything had already been said by his fists.

"I'll have the law on you," said Kenny in a whisper, watching for a new attack.

"You'll have to wite a while, mitey," said the gunner. "There ain't much law in Ireland at present."

Again there was silence. Then Kenny started off on a long, bitter monologue which seemed sometimes to be addressed to Pat and sometimes to himself. His face was as devoid of expression as a bird's, and the words came as if from a dead man.

"I was never meant for this place. The ignorant, primitive people, and the climate here in winter—you only see it in summer. You have no idea what it's like. And I never had your enthusiasm for healing the sick. That will wear off you in time, too. Take my word for it, medicine is a business. Diagnose what the patient has in his pocket and prescribe accordingly. It's all the same in the end. There's no place for sentimentality in our business, especially with babies. They're two a penny. There's plenty more where they came from, you may take it from me. And they're tougher than you think." He began to revive, and Pat found that his momentary pity for him immediately disappeared.

"Those infants on whose behalf you nearly slaughtered me will live to bury us all. They'll probably dance at your funeral." He stood up, with difficulty. A little of his original precise manner had returned.

"Now I'll ask you both to leave my house. I have work to do here."

Pat could not resist saying:

"I'll report you in Galway for taking morphine."

"They know all about me in Galway," said Kenny contemptuously. "But if you must report try to pick a man who isn't taking it himself."

"Come along, young fellow," said Mitey suddenly, seizing Pat by the arm. " 'E's screwy, and that's the truth. We'll leave 'im to 'is work."

Outside in the evening sunshine, Pat looked in wonder at his bleeding fists. He rubbed his hands together as if he were washing them.

"We'll stop in the bog on the w'y home," said Mitey, "and you can dip them. Bog water is a powerful disinfectant."

Roddy received them with respect. It was clear from his manner that he had heard the noise in the house, for he helped Pat up on to the sidecar as if he were a wounded soldier returning from battle. He even unfolded the ancient, unsavoury rug on which he had been sitting, and tucked it firmly around Pat's knees. Though the evening was cooler now, the slanting sun stared hotly still. Pat hated the hard, prickly rug, matted with sweat from the horse, which usually wore it in cold weather. As they moved away from the house, he edged it gradually aside, but very quietly so that Roddy would not be offended.

Mitey, clinging to the sidecar's rail, kept looking back at the doctor's house as long as it remained in sight. The windows shone like polished copper in the low sunlight. Nothing moved there, except when a flight of swallows landed on the ivy as unconcerned as if the house had been in ruins. Neither Pat nor Roddy turned to look when Mitey told them about the swallows. Roddy said savagely:

"The birds could nest in that fellow's whishker and he'd take no notice. I'm sorry you had your journey for nothing, Patcheen."

Until today, it had been years since Roddy had called Pat by this name. It was the one by which all the people had called him, when he was a small boy running in and out of every kitchen in the town land. Now the single word was able to contain all the sympathy that Roddy could never have expressed. Pat found that he prickled with dislike for that manifestation of sympathy, because of the suggestion implied in it that there was worse misfortune to come. Still he spoke very gently to Roddy, almost casually, as he asked:

"Where would we get another doctor?"

"The doctor in Maam died last week. He was old and anyway, when he was alive the only thing the poor man cared about was the fishing, God be good to him. We have to do most of our own repairs in these parts. If someone gets taken bad, we send him in to the hospital in Galway. If you could get in to Galway, now, you'd surely find a man of knowledge there."

"Then we must get in to Galway."

"Dr. Kenny is a bad case, sure enough," said Roddy after a moment, relaxing his efforts to make the horse trot. "He's been like that with years. He got a fright the year of the bad sickness and he won't come into any house now if he thinks even the cat might have the fever. 'Tis not much loss, though, for he was a terrible bad doctor the best day he ever was. Of course he's a Protestant," said Roddy magnanimously, as if this were a complete excuse. "The father was a kind of a squireen below there near Oughterard, and he made a doctor out of him by main force, for the poor man hadn't a brain to his name. 'T was a cruel thing to do to him, for he might have made a good rate-collector, or an agent, or a bailiff, or any of that class of thing. Ay," said Roddy meditatively, "the father put him into this job himself, and he said he could have got a mule appointed the same day, if he wanted. I'm thinking we might do better under the new government."

"If we don't," said Mitey shortly, "there's a lot of good blood wasted."

The mention of blood reminded him that Pat must wash his hands. They got down off the sidecar and crossed the dry, springy bog until they came to a round hole full of black shining water. Pat dangled his hands in it, and splashed his face, and plunged his hands in again, until his whole mood changed and he felt like a man who has discarded clothes that were infested with lice. Mitey understood this. He made Pat lie on the grass at full length, for five minutes. A short rest when you need it, he said, is better than an hour that you have had to wait for. Roddy observed all this washing from the safety of the road, and made no attempt to join in.

Back on the sidecar again, Pat occupied himself in trying to remember the meagre hints that he had received from the doctor. One thing had been rather reassuring, and that was Kenny's conviction of the indestructibility of babies. He had said, too, that there was some sense in the cure of eggs. Pat hugged these pearls of wisdom to him in the same spirit as might have encouraged an ancient Roman returning from a visit to that cross-grained old trollop at Delphi. Many a Roman must have felt like clouting her head for her, as Pat had done to Kenny. He smiled a great, satisfied, uncontrollable smile at the thought of what he had done to Kenny.

They drifted back and forth to the rhythm of the jogging sidecar, their heads bent silently against the dust as if it had been rain. Passing Cáit Conneeley's whitewashed cottage, covered with great splashes of strong pink roses, the children all lined up to stare, so that it was plain enough that the news had been talked over in their hearing. Cáit herself came to lean over the half-door and wave to them. She hooted to Roddy, but her young sheep-dog came galloping around the corner of the house just then and drowned her words with his barking.

They drove slowly up the front avenue and found the same group sitting there on the steps as if they had not moved since they had seen the sidecar off down the avenue an hour and a half before.

# CHAPTER XIII

Since the sun had moved around, the stone-floored drawing-room was cool. Ruth lay slackly on the sofa, still feeling the glow of Colman's presence beside her, although he had gone out on to the steps as soon as he had heard the sidecar turn in at the gateway. She was as happy as a cat who has just enjoyed an hour's petting from its usually neglectful owner. Like a cat she huddled into herself, trying to prolong the feeling of security which had already begun to fade. It seemed to her that the times when Colman talked freely and unselfconsciously, even when they were alone, were becoming fewer with every week. She had fallen in love with him when his self-confidence was at a low ebb. Then there had never been this top, artificial layer that had to be hacked away before she could reach him. She had found something fascinating and appealing in the contrast between his physical magnificence, clothed in manly tweeds and polished leather, and the shrinking, frightened soul that had then inhabited him.

It was all his father's fault. He had put Colman to work in the factory as a clerk, without authority or standing. An older man, called Edwards, was put in charge of him, as if he had been an imbecile. It was a pity that Edwards, since the age of fifteen, when he had entered the firm as an office-boy, had nursed the hope that he would one day see his name on the firm's writing-paper, as a director. Andrews and Edwards, it was to be. He had often written it out in his flowing, clerkly hand at home in his Mount Street lodgings, to see how it would look. Naturally Colman's existence was a thorn in his spare flesh. He lost no opportunity of belittling him, and had even educated the workmen in the factory to do the same. He had a way of saying: "Master Colman," with a little, high, short laugh, immediately smothered, that was more effective than any words could have been. And he complained consistently of Colman's inefficiency. His father co-operated in this persecution, by lazily believing the complaints without sufficiently investigating them.

Ruth was the person who had put a stop to it. Colman poured it all out to her one afternoon in the MacAuleys' drawing-room, which he had taken to haunting when he should have been at work. First, she made him go back to the office and sit down at his desk. Then she went to her father and told him the whole story. She deliberately represented Colman as a strong man whose patience was being tried dangerously far, instead of as the querulous, complaining, down-trodden worm that he was. Her father, who liked nothing better than helping young people, marched into battle against Colman's father. The result was that Colman got an office of his own, with a secretary, and the heading on the writing-paper was changed to Andrews and Son. Edwards was left to bite his nails in the big outer office. Some months later he was run over by the tram outside his own door, and most fortunately killed.

This was three years ago and Ruth had spent the time between in building up Colman's belief in himself. The strange thing was that her own modesty prevented her from seeing what she had achieved. Edwards's death was a help, though she had been hard put to it to persuade Colman to go to the funeral. He came to see her almost every day, and it never occurred to her that during these visits herself had taught him the neat philosophy with which he controlled his mind, and which sometimes exasperated her so much. Neither did she properly realize that a man who from the age of twenty to twenty-three had allowed himself to be held in bondage by his father's clerk could not be very intelligent. Instead she rejoiced when he began to take control of her. She did not like managing women. Although she was by then in love with him, she would not ever have agreed to marry him if she had thought that she was to spend the rest of her life in directing his activities. She prayed for him a great deal and always tried not to be cleverer than he was in company.

Always over-sympathetic of Colman's difficulties, Ruth felt that it was natural for a man who had passed through such a painful time to be absorbed in himself and his own feelings. Still she wished that he could sometimes listen to her troubles, too. Incautiously she had consulted her mother about it, and half-jokingly quoted the remark of an aged French nun at her school, on the question of husbands:

"How he treats the cat he will treat you. Watch the cat."

Colman had no time for cats.

But her mother had urged her to marry him, and though Ruth had already decided to do this, she had an unpleasant sensation of being impelled into marriage. She had got the impression that her mother thought one husband was much the same as another, and that though she did not particularly admire Colman, still she thought him an adequate husband for Ruth. She had seemed inordinately pleased at the idea of Ruth's marriage almost as if she had thought of it until then as an unlikely prospect. So the conversation had only succeeded in hurting Ruth more, and thenceforward she had always felt like calling everyone to admire Colman, whenever he did her a real kindness. He never failed in conventional politeness.

This was why she had been so very pleased when he had come to look for her in the little room where the babies were. He had drawn her away from the cradles, into which she had been staring futilely, and turned her towards the dim green light to examine her face. He said she looked wretched, and he went and found Sarah and brought her in, looking very concerned and anxious about Ruth. Then he made her come and lie on the drawing-room sofa, and sat with her for almost an hour, stroking her hands and her hair, leaning against her half-bare arm with his tweedy shoulder that still smelt of turf smoke from the weaver's room in which the cloth had been made. Gradually a warm current had begun to flow through her, reducing pleasantly her understanding and sense of responsibility, as if she were drunk. The prolonging of this state of physical contentment became so important to her that she resented Pat's return. She heard him get down slowly from the sidecar and walk up the steps, and sit down among the others to tell his story. It was their shocked exclamations that brought her drowsily to her feet. She came out through the front doorway to hear Colman blustering, in a tone she knew would annoy Pat:

"I wouldn't have let him get away with simply refusing to come. I'd have taught him a lesson he wouldn't forget."

Pat said calmly:

"Well, I did hit him on the head with a chair."

Nora gave her little delighted shriek of laughter. Colman turned towards her a look of dislike that immediately swallowed up all of Ruth's precarious happiness. It was as if a pit full of little, writhing devils had opened silently and suddenly at her feet. Now, horribly and clearly, she saw that Colman's attentions to her for the last hour had been primarily for his own comfort. Needing a respite from the prevailing gloom, he had pretended to be concerned about her, so that he could sit and talk to her and play with her for a while. Now she began to remember a curiously hard, determined note in his voice when he had conducted Sarah into the little room. It was Sarah, of course, who had had to pay for his amusement. She almost panicked at the sudden thought that he might have said something harsh to Sarah. Standing on the doorstep, very still, she longed to rush away to Sarah and make amends. But this would amount to denouncing Colman and she could not bring herself to do it. She looked across at him, arrogant and tiresomely stuffy, but so dependent on her that she knew she would never abandon him now.

Kate called them in to supper before they had time for any more discussion. She had a salmon of which she was very proud.

"I got a couple of the lads in the yard to lift him out of the river for me. Miss Sharman won't know a bit about it, so she won't lose no sleep."

Miss Sharman was the almost mythical owner of the fishing rights of the river which flowed into the sea, between high rocky banks, a mile west of Derrylea. She never came to Ireland, and it is hard to respect the property of someone you have never seen. The local men with considerable delicacy usually confined their poaching to the night-time. Recognizing the present emergency, however, they had shown the two military men where to find the salmon on a hot day, and had helped them to land several fish, so that there was salmon for supper in the yard, too.

Things were not so black in other ways, said Kate, standing chattily in the dining-room doorway. She had three pairs of young cocks marching around the yard this minute without the smallest suspicion of what was in store for them.

"And Hannah Frank has ducks that she was going to bring to the market in Galway in a fortnight's time, and sure, she might as well give them to us as to some total stranger that mightn't appreciate them. And I'm sending Roddy back with the sidecar now to Kelly's shop for some flour, and to say it's for your mother, so maybe they'll spare us a bit if they can. And Fahy's promised us flake meal, and I'll be able to hold them to that."

Already exhausted from the heat as well as from the anxieties of the day, this gargantuan recital had the effect of destroying the last of Ruth's appetite. The others ate voraciously but automatically. Even Brian was absent-minded. He had slipped in at the last moment and sat quite silent all during the meal. Ruth felt sorry for him. He had been neglected by everyone all day, and no one had bothered even to tell him the news about the doctor, when he had come in. Still she was so oppressed with her own troubles that she could not start a conversation with him. When he had finished he got up and went out again, and no one thought of asking him to stay for the conference that they all knew must come now.

They were on their way across the hall to the drawing-room when Joe said:

"We must decide at once what is to be done next."

Colman stopped and turned towards the front door.

"I'm afraid I can't offer any advice," he said, apparently in genuine distress at his inadequacy. "I'll just go out for a short walk while you talk it over. Coming, Ruth?"

"No!" said Ruth sharply, taken by surprise. She added lamely: "I'll come to the gate with you."

When they had gone out, Nora said:

"I'll fetch Sarah."

She could not conceal her pleasure in Colman's departure. Through the open door of the drawing-room, Pat and Joe heard her skipping off down the corridor. Automatically they ranged chairs around the empty hearth and sat down opposite each other. Suddenly Pat remembered that he had promised to close the attic window at sundown.

"I did it," said Joe. "He asked me to, when I went to see him. He's cooler this evening, I think."

"Thank God," said Pat fervently. "When I left him today I thought he was going to be my first murder."

"Nice of you to take the blame, old man," said Joe. "I looked at his knee, and there's no swelling, no purple spots."

"Kenny said he probably has typhoid as well. That was his main reason for not coming. It was extraordinary how he just sat there and let me hit him. Still there was great satisfaction in it."

"I spent enough of my childhood in this part of the world to know typhoid when I see it," said Joe. "That man hasn't got any signs of typhoid. He's not even shivering. Kenny is a half-lunatic, of course. I had no hopes of him. But I don't think it will be much use getting anyone else either." Seeing Pat's shocked expression he went on quickly, looking down at his toes: "It's no use trying to get to Clifden. Horgan says there's fighting up that way today. We'd only be turned back. So Galway by boat is the only chance. That would be two days, one day to go and one to come. By then I think it may be too late."

"Too late? Already?"

"Every time I look at Paul, he's worse. You'll see."

"But Kenny says babies are tough. He doesn't expect them to die."

123

"But they do. He has often seen it."

"We can't stop trying to get a doctor. It's madness to give up. We can't just do nothing."

"No, I suppose we can't," said Joe, after a moment. "Which of us is going to go in the boat for the doctor, supposing that Horgan lets one of us go?"

"Neither of us could manage here alone. Don't forget the man in the attic. And the column in the yard. And if things go wrong, there will be complications——"

At the same moment they both thought of Colman. It was a delightful solution. Joe laughed, a little slow, soft laugh like a clucking hen. Then they looked at each other guiltily.

" 'T would be a blessing from God to get that man out of the house," said Joe then. "You'd think he doesn't know what's happening at all, or that if he does know, he doesn't care a damn."

"But when he has children of his own I bet he'll be like a tigress with her young," said Pat bitterly. "I shouldn't speak about Ruth's future husband like that." Joe started to say something, but thought better of it. Pat went on, as flatly as he could: "Anyway, if either of those children is going to die, we'll be glad not to have Colman about the place, saying all the wrong things and upsetting everyone. The only thing is, how will Ruth get on without him?"

"Much better," said Joe emphatically. "He makes her self-conscious about her misfortunes. At least he did this afternoon while you were out. Took her away from her job, made an invalid of her——"

Nora and Sarah were at the door, and Ruth a step behind them, having seen Colman to the gate and run all the way back for fear of again neglecting her duty. They pulled the chairs in to a smaller ring and spoke in low tones, as if they feared that they would be overheard. Sarah approved of the idea of trying to get a message in to Galway by boat.

"There's Martin Faherty will bring it if I ask him—that's Mary Tommy's young man. They're to be married on Tuesday, but he'll be glad enough to be away for a few days first." She offered no explanation of why he would be glad, though Joe raised an eyebrow at her. "And he can take Gander with him, and Mr. Andrews, and they'll manage the boat fine between them." Colman was the only one of the party that she spoke of thus formally. "There's only one thing. Martin nor Gander—the devil wouldn't get a word out of either of them. But is there any fear that Mr. Andrews would tell people in Galway about the men out in the yard?"

"We'll warn him about that," said Ruth. "There will be no need for him to mention them to anyone. He can just find a doctor and get him into the boat and bring him here."

It did not sound an easy task, as she said it. Sarah and Joe glanced quickly at each other. Joe said:

"I'll fix it with Horgan, if I can. He may refuse to let us send a boat to Galway."

"He can't," said Nora sharply. "When you tell him how ill the babies are, he must let us send for help."

"Well, I'll do what I can," said Joe. "Come along, Sarah. You might be better able to persuade him than I could."

# CHAPTER XIV

Out in the hall, with the drawing-room door shut behind them, Sarah said explosively:

"In the name of God, what do they think the doctor is going to do if he comes?"

"It gives them something to hope for."

"And what doctor is going to leave his business in Galway and climb into a hooker and sail out to the back of Connemara?"

"It's a doctor's business to go when he's called. Besides," Joe suggested, "they might do it for Colman, when they wouldn't do it for you or me."

" 'Tis true for you, he's a great man to give orders," said Sarah. "Though that's not always the best way to get people to do a thing for you."

"Who is with the children now?"

"Hannah Frank. She came over a small while ago to help me. 'T was decent out of her to come, but she has such lamentations that she makes things a lot harder to put up with. My mother will be down later on, though, and she'll put a stop to her."

They looked into the little room before going out to the yard. Hannah was there in almost total darkness, on her knees praying aloud, extempore:

"Holy Mary, that was a mother yourself, let you not afflict the poor woman now with her children dying on her, for that's the worst misfortune that can fall on any woman, as you ought to know yourself from the day long ago when you lost your own little boy for three whole days, and I'm sure you cried your eyes down and you the mother of God itself. . . ."

They slipped away again without speaking to her, but passing through the kitchen Joe told Kate to bring her a lamp from the collection standing ready filled on the kitchen table. The range was still pouring out heat, like molten lava, into the room. The back door was standing open, to let in the cool night air. Soft sounds of movement could be heard from out there, as some of the men walked about for exercise. At the far end of the yard they could see in the dusk that a little group was gathered around one man who had a tin whistle on which he was playing "The Blackbird". The soft, round, slightly hesitant notes might but for their rhythm have come from a real blackbird. One man started a step of the hornpipe on the cobbles, found them too rough and moved in on to the flagged coach-house floor to continue it. When he had finished the man with the whistle started a melancholy tune like a slow march. The audience sighed appreciatively. Very softly, from the back of the group, came a high, thin, tenor voice, singing:

*"Oh, wrap the green flag round me, boys:*
*To die were far more sweet,*
*With Erin's glorious emblem, boys,*
*To be my winding sheet."*

Horgan was talking earnestly to three other men, at the near end of the yard. When he saw Joe and Sarah standing in the doorway, he crossed to them quickly. Sarah said sharply:

"You said there would be no singing."

"They must keep their heart up," said Horgan. "And anyway, there's no one within miles to hear them."

"Except us," said Sarah.

"A bit of a song never hurt anyone. Are ye wanting something? Don't come out here unless it's for something important."

"When are ye going?"

"Maybe tomorrow, maybe the day after. We're all right here," said Horgan, teasing her.

"You heard the doctor wouldn't come," said Joe hurriedly.

"Mitey told me." He sounded uninterested, impatient, even bored.

"Well, now we want to send a boat in to Galway for a doctor."

"I'm not sending Mitey to Galway. He's well known there."

"You needn't send Mitey. Two local men will go, and Mr. Andrews, the big fellow that's with us."

The men at the far end of the yard had begun to whistle at Sarah. A remark or two floated up to them:

"There's hope for the country yet."

"I say she ought to be nationalized."

"I wonder would it be any good asking her to join the column?"

Horgan turned his back on them and said:

"Can't you wait until we move on? We'd be gone long ago only for the man upstairs. If he's not on his feet by tomorrow evening we'll have to go without him."

"We don't want him, faith," said Sarah with a snort. "You'd best make up your mind to take him along with you."

"Tomorrow evening may be too late," said Joe. "You know the people of Ireland are not all over-thankful to your crowd for keeping the war going just when they thought they were finished with wars. If it comes out that you wouldn't let a houseful of youngsters send for the doctor for a couple of dying babies, you'll be even more unpopular. It's the very thing that will catch the public imagination. Whether you win or lose, you'll never live it down."

"Babies always come badly out of wars," said Horgan bitterly. "You ought to know that. Sentimentality has lost many a war for Ireland."

He started to tell the story of the trainload of Black and Tans that had got away on the Dingle line, because a message had come to say that there were three nuns on the train also. In the middle of this, a commotion started up at the other end of the yard. The men's attention had been diverted from Sarah to a little, bent old man who came slithering through the wicket-gate, hotly pursued by an indignant sentry. Horgan marched down the yard, followed more slowly by the three men to whom he had been talking earlier. Sarah started to follow, too, but Joe held her back with a hand on her arm.

"What's this? Who's this man?"

The sentry jumped in his skin at Horgan's tone, which seemed to cut through his clothes like a whiplash. He waggled apologetically.

"It's an old Fenian, sir, that said he wanted to be talking to the boys. Someone told him we're here——"

"Why did you let him in?"

"Because I couldn't keep him out, sir. He just kept slipping out of my hand and running on a bit. When I'd catch him he'd just do the same again. I'm hampered with the gun, you see."

"Hampered!"

Soldierly words cannonaded from the ancient stone walls of the yard. The sentry crouched and said. "Ah, now, Captain. Ah, now, Captain!" The rest of the men chuckled and moved closer to enjoy the fun. A voice chanted derisively, from the back:

> "*That's the stuff to give the troops,*
> *Linseed meal and castor oil!*"

Horgan stopped and breathed hard, like a bull about to charge. Then he said softly:

"And tell me now, sonny, why didn't you lift your little gun to your shoulder and shoot?"

The last word was a roar that made the sentry bite his tongue in fright. When he could speak, he said in horrified accents:

"But, Captain, how could I shoot an old man, a Fenian too, that spent seven years in an English jail——"

"If you had shot him first he wouldn't have had time to tell you how many years he spent in jail. Hampered, faith! Running after him like a kid playing tig! Get out there to your beat and don't forget the next time what you have that gun for."

He watched the sentry scuttle out of the yard as if there were tigers after him. Then he turned to the old man who had been an interested and approving observer of the scene, and said roughly:

"Where are you from?"

"Over by Recess, Captain," said the man, in a soft, drawling voice. "I heard the boys were here and I walked over to have a chat with them."

"You heard about us in Recess!"

"Sure, of course, The whole country is talking about ye, after the explosions yesterday. The wife didn't want me to come down at all. She's always afraid someone will catch a hold of me again and put me back in jail, and then there'd be no one to earth up to the spuds for her. That's what I came talking to ye about. Let ye be going home now while ye have the chance. That's what Michael Davitt always said: 'Keep a firm grip on your homesteads.' Them was his words. I saw Swansea and Cardiff and Bermingham and London. All those places. And I can swear to you, there's no place like home, if we only had a decent bite to eat."

"What were you in jail for, Daddy?" the singer asked, not altogether derisively.

" 'T was over an eviction, Sonny, below near Ough-terard. I was staying with the uncle. His neighbour was being evicted, a decent, soft kind of a man with about eleven children."

"A hard kind of a man, I'd call him," said the singer solemnly.

131

"Faith and you would not", said the old man, "if you saw him there in the middle of all the children and he crying away as bad as any of them. Go to America, the landlord said to him, and he knowing well that that man couldn't buy a jacket for a gooseberry, let alone thirteen passages to America. The wife was a fine girl, though. She's dead since, the Lord be merciful to her. Piled the dresser and the kitchen table and the beds and the cradle up behind the door, she did, so that the Peelers had to get a battering-ram to break it down. I came along and they hard at it, myself and the uncle and a few more of the neighbours. I got one of the R.I.C.'s by the tail of his coat, and then I got a hold of the tail of himself. We had little small knives like you'd use to carve out a pair of oars for a currach. I gave him mine in the seat of his pants, like you'd spear a fish. I'm telling you he dropped that battering-ram bloody quick. But like that in the old song, they were ten to one. And they had guns, too. Sure they had the lot of us captured while you'd be saying cush to a duck. The last thing we saw was the gable wall coming down. That was a thing to make a man fight until the life would drop out of him."

The drawling, half-humorous voice paused. The men were silent now, deeply moved at this personal and terribly clear little picture, which still lived for the old man as if it had happened yesterday.

The singer started again:

> "Oh, *wrap the green flag round me, boys,*
> *To die were far more sweet——*"

"Green flags aren't half as important as people," the

old man interrupted. "I'll sing you a better song." He cleared his throat loudly. " 'Tis about an eviction. A terrible sad song. The wife won't let me sing it at home, for it's too lonesome. But I often sing it for myself and I out in the fields."

"Earthing up to the spuds," said the singer, who had not been pleased at being cut short.

The old man began his song, quite unperturbed.

"*Our mountain streams were rushing, Annie dear.*
*The autumn woods were blushing, Annie dear.*
*But brighter was your blushing,*
*When first your murmurs hushing,*
*I told my love out-gushing,*
  *Annie dear.*"

He was very short of breath but his voice was clear and strong. Like all Connemara singers, he fixed his eye on a high distant point as he sang, so that his chin came up, while he swayed back and forth on his feet with a kind of conventional, unfelt embarrassment. He was a natural artist. He quickened the tempo when the song described the burning of the little cottage, and then let it drop away slowly at the end, so that the full beauty of the melody appeared:

"*Far better by you lying,*
 *Than live an exile sighing,*
  *Annie dear.*"

Tears rolled down his cheeks and his voice broke on the last notes. His sincerity had invested the self-con-

133

scious words with passionate feeling. One of the men said:

"That's a fine song, to be sure."

"The land and the people," said the old man eagerly, "they're the only things worth fighting for. Don't forget that."

"There's something in the old flag, too," said Mitey. "I wouldn't know what to do with a bit of land now, if I got it."

"Sentimentality has lost many a war for Ireland," said Joe softly in Horgan's ear.

"We're all in it for the old flag," said another man. "The day I saw the flag of Ireland trailed in the mud through Galway City at the back of a lorry of Black and Tans, I'd have done murder and that's God's truth. That's why I'm here."

The singer started again:

*"Up de Valera! He's the champion in the right.*
*We'll follow him to battle in the orange, green, and white."*

Every voice joined in the last line, sharp and clear:

*"And we'll crown de Valera king of Ireland!"*

"Holy smoke!" said Joe. "King of Ireland!"

"It's all right," said Horgan sardonically. "In another place it says: 'We want a republic for Ireland.'"

The old man was saying:

"Ay, de Valera is a good young fellow, and a man of education too. Now Michael Davitt wasn't a man of education, but John Redmond was——"

Immediately someone started another verse of the same song:

"*When we were little children, John Redmond was a fool,*
  *He thought we would be satisfied with something called*
    *Home Rule,*
  *But we have learned a thing or two since we've attended*
    *school,*
  *And we want a Republic for Ireland.*"

Before they could start up the chorus again, Mitey laid a soothing hand on the shoulder of the old man, who was now prancing with temper at the brushing aside of his heroes.

"We all have the sime idea, mitey. Get the country to ourselves and we'll mike our own arringements. It's only a question of how you go about it."

Suddenly Sarah lost her patience. She darted forward and seized Horgan by the arm and shook him passionately.

"Are we going to stand here listening to this kind of thing all night? Don't you care anything at all for that poor woman's children, that you won't even listen to us telling you about them? Come on away and leave them to their singing. I think it's the way you're not able to stop them."

Horgan shook her off roughly, angry at the grins of his men. The nearest ones, who had heard what she said, herded the others into the coach-house doorway. Here they all sat on the ground, leaning against each other, as if they were gathered at a cross-roads in peacetimes to watch the girls walk nervously by. Since there were no girls to amuse them here they went on with their concert.

The old man squatted in front of them. He seemed to have no intention of going back to his wife, as long as he could stay here and cry his fill over the bad old times. The man with the tin whistle was out in front too, filling in the gaps between the songs with jigs and hornpipes.

Horgan hurried off up the yard towards the back door of the house as if it had been his own idea that they should get away from interrruptions to discuss the question of the boat. He led the way into the kitchen. The room was dimly lit now by a single oil-lamp that hung by the fireplace. There was no sign of Kate. With an emphatic clatter he pulled out a chair and planted himself in it at the head of the table, Sarah and Joe sat one at either side of him. Throughout their discussion, they could hear the men outside singing emigrant songs— *The Old Bog-Road* and *The County of Mayo*, and then from the old man a vibrant solo that went:

> "*What will I do, love, when you are going,*
> *With white sails flowing to the seas beyond?*
> *What will I do, love, when waves divide us,*
> *And friends may chide us for being fond?*"

At the moment of turning to follow Horgan, Joe had noticed that Brian had appeared from the darkness of the coach-house interior, and was settling down among the men. He saw that they made room for him as casually as if he were one of themselves.

# CHAPTER XV

It was plain from the start that Horgan was uneasy. Sarah despised him for this. Above all things she admired a man who was decisive, even if he decided wrongly. She might have teased him a little anyway, in her anger with him for having to be consulted at all. Now seeing his weakness, savagely she enjoyed baiting him with derisive remarks about the apparent lack of military discipline in his little column. At first Horgan reacted entirely to her satisfaction. He drew his heavy black eyebrows together and stuck out his lower jaw so that he looked like a disgruntled monkey. Joe found it extremely difficult to control his irritation with Sarah's heavy, Connemara sarcasm. Since the first twelve years of his life had been spent in this place, he knew the idiom as well as she did. But she was his only ally and support, and he would not risk even the mildest disagreement with her in Horgan's presence. Then, unexpectedly, Horgan's sense of humour seemed to return.

"I'd swear you're getting fond of me, Sarah," he said mockingly.

Sarah flushed with annoyance, all the deeper because she had never practised the common trick of attempting to attract attention by means of abuse and insults. The Captain surveyed her for a long moment, with one eyebrow raised in amusement, while he savoured to the full the restoration of his self-respect. Then with a tiny, leisurely turn of his shoulder away from her, he indicated that his conversation was going to be addressed to Joe. Sarah was relieved at this. She knew now that she was no match for Horgan and that she should not have tried to subdue him. And in his very first words he used her comments to support his own argument:

"I know my men don't look a bit like soldiers. There's no one knows it better. I often think of what the Duke of Wellington said to his own bunch the day long ago: 'I don't know what the enemy will think of you, but by God you frighten me.'"

Joe chuckled. Horgan went on quickly:

"But that's only the look of them. They're fine for guerrilla warfare, and that's what it will be now. From now on the first thing will be secrecy. And hardheartedness. Ruthlessness. We can't afford to be romantic and sentimental. We'll have to go back to the tactics we used in the Black and Tan times. That was Tom Barry's principle—to be cleverer and tougher than the enemy. If we're not we may as well give up before we start!"

"Were you in the Black and Tan war?" Joe asked with interest.

"I was a local intelligence officer," said Horgan. "I know that's not the best way to learn military tactics. But I have a brother that was in the British Army. He's in Boston now. He used to bring home manuals about what they did in the Boer War. You'd be surprised what you'd learn from books like that. I wish to God we had a few professional soldiers to fall back on," he burst out with sudden savagery. "Only for Mitey we'd all be behind barbed wire long ago."

"Revolutions are usually worked by amateurs," said Joe drily. "In downtrodden countries men don't gain military experience unless they're on the wrong side. Besides not to know the rules of the game can sometimes be a great help. And it leaves room for charity——"

"Ah, to hell with charity," said Horgan. "That's only another word for sentimentality. It's all blather and talk. Everyone from here to Recess is talking about us—you heard the old man say that. What chance have we of conducting a war when the people aren't afraid of us? From now on we'll have to show that we're serious. They'll have to see we're in earnest. We went soft during the Truce. We'll have to go back to burning houses and shooting spies." He bounded to his feet and walked up and down the kitchen, with a strange prancing gait as if the floor were burning the soles of his feet.

"And that means no boat goes in to Galway. We'll be needing some of those boats ourselves, maybe, and the rest of them are going to be put out of action."

Joe sat very still, careful not to show any sign of being infected with Horgan's excitement. Then he said flatly:

"Your main trouble is that your enemy has learned all the tricks in the same way as you have. Of course it's nothing to do with me. As far as I'm concerned, one lot of you is as bad as the other and a damned sight worse. But I can't help thinking that it would serve your country better if you'd put all this energy into building up something new and good. That's what the ordinary people of the country want."

"The ordinary people will thank us afterwards for saving the soul of the country for them. And you can't build on rotten foundations."

There was a short pause, and then Joe said:

"It's harder to stop people from fighting than it is to start them. That's why you have a civil war on your hands at all."

Seeing the expression of a wronged idealist spread over Horgan's face, Joe gave up the attempt to move him by shaking his faith in himself and his cause. He tried another approach.

"It would be good policy for you to let us send in to Galway for a doctor. You'd get a lot of cheap credit for it."

"Cheap romantic credit," said Horgan with contempt. "That's not the kind of credit we need just now."

"So there's going to be no more respect for people's feelings," said Joe slowly. "Maybe you're right. Still, you must admit that the people who started this revolution were as romantic a collection as you'd hope to find —poets, several of them. Maybe you'll say that's why they failed. They certainly didn't know much about the technicalities of war. But Tom Barry, your ruthless man, he didn't fail, though he was a romantic, too. You can't deny that. I'm sure you heard how he brought a bagpiper to play at the Crossbarry ambush, because he wanted to find out whether the Irish fight better to the sound of pipe music. The poor old enemy must have thought they were in a madhouse."

Horgan was listening to him now, all right. Joe went on carefully, not hurrying to press his advantage.

"When the Irish accept a purely materialistic point of view that's when the soul of the country will be lost. Maybe you're right in tightening things up, but a mixture of romanticism is necessary too. I was with a romantic woman in 1916, and for us she was Queen Maeve and Granuaile and Mother Eire all rolled into one. Of course I was only seventeen then, but the other Fianna boys felt the same. Any of us would have died for her. Some of us did. Do you think we could have felt like that if we had viewed things in the light of reason? Countess Markievicz never bothers about difficulties. Even some of her friends said she was reckless. It is quite certain that anyone who followed her took his life in his hands. But we never gave a thought to that. We might have, if reason had been the standard."

"I don't value my own life all that high," said Horgan, moving slowly back to his chair at the top of the table.

"I know you don't," said Joe gently. "Indeed, I was about to point out that the less you value your own life the less you are likely to value the lives of other people —civilians, women, children and all. Our lot didn't make that mistake. Well, they failed, you may say. Perhaps they did. Their picture of war was full of old-fashioned, bookish ideas about chivalry, and they never changed until they were all dead. But everything is different now. I know you are right about that. Civil war is a bitter, evil thing in itself. It's not likely to generate chivalry. Good can't come out of evil."

"If you hadn't been with the Countess in 1916 I'd knock your teeth down your throat for that," said Horgan, in a tone of bewilderment.

Joe prayed that Sarah would still be silent. He caught her eye, and saw by her very lack of expression that she understood how near they were to victory. Horgan made one last half-hearted attempt to keep his mastery of the situation.

"It's a queer thing", he said uneasily, "how you could be out in 1916, and have no hand, act nor part in the Tan war, nor in the Civil War afterwards."

Sarah could not forbear from snorting. Joe said quickly, almost apologetically:

"Well, there was the year in camp in Frongoch after 1916. Then when we were all let out in 1917 they made me a headquarter's messenger That meant, of course, that I could have nothing to do with the military side. I was only useful as long as I was not known. I'm not really much of a fighting man, in any case. Too small, I suppose."

"And the other young lad, MacAuley, was he in it too?"

"He was too young," said Joe. "And, anyway, his people weren't in the movement at all, though they were always sympathetic. It was my father brought me into it. He fought in the General Post Office in 1916——"

This was the end of Horgan's resistance, of course. Afterwards, Joe felt a little mean about it. He had not intended to collapse the unfortunate Captain so thoroughly. Neither had he been in the least cynical in giving an account of his own military history. Horgan never suspected him of cynicism however. And he kept his dignity, too, even in the midst of his apologies. Before he gave his formal permission for a boat to be taken to Galway, he explained as well as he could why his attitude had changed:

"I was one of those slow fellows that didn't join in anything until after the Rising was over. It wasn't that I didn't know what was going on. But I was slow to make up my mind, and I'm sorry every day since. I'd give my eye even to have seen Pearse, or any of them. He used to spend his holidays over by Gortmore. He had a little house there. I could have met him, lots of times. But I threw away the chance," he said disconsolately, "and how can I lay down the law now to one that wasn't so damn cautious? You can take a boat, if you like. I suppose you'll warn that west British yoke that's going on it to keep his mouth shut about us in Galway."

So Horgan hadn't taken to Colman either, thought Joe with interest. He thanked him without warmth and then they sat in silence for a few minutes. The song that came from outside now brought a heavy sense of pain and loss to Joe. It was not a good song, but it had been the favourite marching song in Dublin six years ago, when all their hopes were artificially high and before any blood had been spilt. It was an emigrant song, too, and even while it refreshed intolerable memories for him, Joe wondered at the huge repertoire of these that the men could summon up. These songs were the favourite entertainment at American wakes, as the party on the eve of emigration was called.

To return from America was almost impossible. As

Hannah Frank had said, rearing children in Connemara was like rearing turkeys for the Christmas market. It was dim comfort indeed to receive after a while unnatural photographs of strange young people with alien faces, dressed in peculiar American clothes. Fathers and brothers set to work to make large fretwork frames for them, so that they could take their place on the mantelshelf and gradually fade into ghosts, from the heat and the acid turf dust continually drifting over them. Parcels of odd, unwearable clothes arrived too, and money, and letters with news of success or failure. That was all. Down through the years of exile the same wailing, discouraging songs would ring in the ears of the emigrants, as if the people who were left behind were determined to make them suffer for their decision to go. The song that reached the group in the dim kitchen now was one of the few that had come back across the Atlantic:

> *Deep in Canadian woods we've met,*
> *From one bright island flown.*
> *Great is the land we tread, but yet,*
> *Our hearts are with our own.*

As they all thundered out the chorus Horgan gave a dismayed exclamation:

"They'll rouse the whole country-side!" And he pushed back his chair so violently that it fell clattering on the floor, and darted out into the yard.

Joe and Sarah grinned at each other uneasily across the table, uncertain of what it was that they had accomplished. Then Joe said:

"I'll tell the others that the boat can go. You can go back to the children now."

As they went towards the door together he held her rigid arm gently as if it were necessary to show her the way. After he had left her she wept bitterly to herself all the way along the corridor to the little room, wandering crazily from wall to wall. At the door she paused and stretched her arms wide. She was surprised to find that the pain in her heart was a little less fierce now, so that she was able to walk quietly into the room and shut the door softly and slowly behind her.

# CHAPTER XVI

Colman had come back from his walk and was sitting with the others in the drawing-room when Joe came in. He seemed anxious to make amends for having deserted them and offered some sober and useful advice about the boat. It was he who suggested that they should take a cargo of some sort, so that they would have it to show if they were held up and questioned. The spirits of the three MacAuleys revived a little as they listened to him, for he emanated an air of adult experience which gave them back a feeling of security. Still Pat, with inconvenient clear-sightedness, thought he detected a false note somewhere. He wondered if Ruth had noticed it, too. He thought she was watching Colman a little anxiously. Instead of feeling angry with Colman, Pat found that he was coolly compassionate now since his last conversation with Joe. This feeling was spiritually allied to the detached pity for humanity in general which always possessed him, and which, when he had recognized it, had been one of his proofs that he was born to be a doctor. Now, not for the first time in his life, he wished he were a little less intelligent, a little less perceptive, or at least that he had a lesser sense of responsibility for the behaviour of others. This last seemed to him to be a most unprofitable attitude of mind and was certainly very disturbing.

Joe said:

"We thought you might take charge of the boat, Colman. The local boys might be turned back too easily. I know that one of us should go, because we must have a trustworthy messenger. You are the most knowledgeable about boats. And you have a persuasive way with you, too. You can put it to work on the first good doctor that you meet in Galway."

He smiled his apologies at Colman for deceiving him so callously. Colman's glance had shot across to Ruth and away again.

"How will you get along here, alone?" he asked Joe.

"Don't forget that this is my native country," said Joe, playing the part of the brave boy who stays behind to protect the ladies while his father goes off to shoot bears.

"Yes, of course. I had forgotten," said Colman hastily and in embarrassment at having so clumsily reminded Joe of his humble origins.

Joe looked quickly across at Pat and shook his head very slightly, admonishing him to swallow his anger. Colman was saying:

"Yes, I'll certainly be able to help with the boat, though I've never before sailed so far in a hooker."

He owned a twenty-ton yacht at Dun Laoghaire and was an expert sailor.

"Gander and Martin Faherty will sail the boat," said Nora. "You won't have to worry about that."

"Thank you, I wasn't," said Colman, in a hard tone.

"We had to promise the Captain that nothing would be said in Galway about the column," said Joe. "I only mention it because he may say something to you about it himself. He seems touchy. He has to be, with his responsibilities."

After that there was no more conversation until they drifted away to bed. Without intending to, their little group had broken up into separate entities. Whatever solidarity they had had as a group was gone. Each of them was suffering so intensely and so differently that there was no question of one being able to comfort another. Still Ruth brought Nora in to sleep in her room, because she saw the desperation in her face as they were about to part at the top of the stairs. Nora came eagerly with her. She had been watching all day for a kind word from Ruth, and now it had come just when she needed it most. Joe had sent Sarah away to bed and was spending the night in the little room with the babies. Nora had intended to creep down and stay with him for a while, but she was glad enough not to be able to do that. She did not want to see the babies now. Even to think of them made her clench her teeth and squeeze her hands tightly shut to stop the tingling horror in her fingers from creeping through and through her.

It did not occur to her that Ruth needed her company. In fact Ruth was consumed with self-disgust. Here, in the midst of this crisis, she was utterly unable to feel for anyone but herself. Since Pat's return from his useless visit to the doctor, she had gone about in a half-dream from which she seemed to awaken now and then with a sensation of falling. It was Colman and fear for Colman that filled her thoughts. There was no reason why this should be. He was there before her eyes. Every time she looked quickly for him, he was watching her, ready to smile a reply. But each time she expected to find that he had vanished. She could not understand it. Little by little her nerves were being ground away. She knew that if she were not a monster of selfishness, all this should be suffered for the babies, or even for Nora. But it was not. It was for herself, no matter how she struggled. She longed to talk to Nora about Colman but she knew that it would be wrong to do so, even though she was her sister.

In the morning it was a relief to them all to plan and do something real. Joe had not slept at all, so he claimed the privilege of walking in the fresh morning air to borrow a boat and collect a crew for it. He took Nora with him. Sarah's mother had come, as she had promised, and had spent the night in preparing infinitesimal meals of arrowroot and a kind of jelly that she made from barley. She and Joe had fed these to the children at intervals. They offered no information to the others about the events of the night.

Brian made an excuse to go out early to the yard and did not come back. The others were rather pleased at this. They took it as a sign that he did not feel much concerned in the family crisis, and that he could still enjoy himself in a boy's way with the excitement of the column.

Ruth had to spend the morning in the kitchen, because Kate did not come. This had never happened before. Sarah ran up to find out if she were ill and was met by a defiant Kate at the door of her cottage, hands on her hips, announcing that she would not work in a fever house. Sarah enjoyed sending her scuttling in behind her slammed door with a cataract of well-chosen Gaelic curses which, if they had worked, would have left the unfortunate Kate bald, toothless and crippled long before her time. But then Sarah had to go back to Ruth with a paraphrased version of Kate's reasons for not coming. Ruth saw through it at once, of course, and this desertion by a woman whom she had never liked, frightened her more than anything else had done. Sarah said briskly:

"We're a lot better off without her. She has no nature in her, that one. My mother will stay here instead of her. Won't you, Mammy?"

"I will that, a-girleen," said her mother, who was making bread at the table as calmly as if she had spent the night at home in bed. "And Hannie Frank will stop here, too. I'll tell her we don't want no ologoning. We'll do a lot more work between us than Kate, and I'm thinking we won't eat the one-half of what she does."

So Ruth went up with Pat to see the man in the attic. She had almost forgotten his existence. Just before they opened the door she was seized with terror lest they might find him dead. That was only for a moment, however, for she saw at once over Pat's shoulder that the patient was sitting up in bed, playing cards with Mitey, who had slipped into the house and up the stairs unnoticed.

"Morning, Pat," said Mitey cheerfully. "I'm giving Dan some of my special treatment."

Dan's long nose and jaw and his slanting, expressionless brown eyes gave him the ingratiating appearance of a second-rate sheepdog. Mitey had brought him a message from the Captain that he was to be ready to march with the column in the evening.

"And sure I'm not able to put a leg under me at all this morning," he said mournfully. "I'm thinking you did a bit of harm yesterday with your little knife."

This was not an accusation but a simple statement which Pat suspected might be all too well-justified.

"Show me that leg," he said sharply.

He took off the bandage as carefully as if he were taking eggs from under a hen, as Dan said admiringly. The wound looked perfectly healthy, though it was plain enough that there could be no question of marching on it. Ruth said, peeping at the bloodstained flesh in well-concealed disgust:

"You must stay here of course. I'll tell the Captain. He'll have to listen to reason."

"The trouble is that I'm the gelignite expert," said Dan modestly. "It was myself that blew up the bridges, there a couple of days ago. You might have heard about it. First there was the big white railway bridge over the Corrib that the train goes over. Maybe you know it? And after, there was the road bridge up at Keel. That was easy, though it was a fine strong bridge in its day. But the big one needed skill, though I say it myself. It isn't everyone that could blow up the big white bridge."

"Were there any bats under it?" Pat asked solemnly.

"Ah, now, you're only making game of me. And sure, how could there be bats when it was all iron slats and bars, and hardly a dark place at all for them to sleep? I do hate bats," he explained kindly to Ruth who was looking at him in dumb horror.

"Where did you learn your trade?" Pat asked, intent on bandaging up the wound again.

"In the quarries," said Dan. "Above on the Screeb road I was working when the Captain was the foreman there. He knows all about gelignite, too, of course, but he can't look after everything at once. He needs me."

"He'll have to do with me now, I'm afraid," said Mitey.

"You have your own job," said Dan. "Me to blow up the barracks and you to shoot the Staters when what's left of them come running out——"

Ruth gave a low, agonized cry. Dan looked at her sorrowfully.

" 'Tis a damn' nasty thing for a nice young girl to hear, and I'm sorry I said it. But I'll tell you, Miss," he said earnestly, fixing his flat brown eyes on her, "them Staters, is a pack of bad bastards."

"Shut yer trap, Dan," said Mitey, with a wail.

Ruth simply turned and ran out of the attic, leaving Dan bleating apologies to Pat.

"I got carried away," he said. "I forgot she was a city lady. And 'tis all only talk anyway, because I know full well that I can't walk. The whole skill in blowing things up is to make sure the charge goes the right way. There's no good in starting to blow up a barracks and ending by blowing the tail-end off of yourself. That's what happens to the other fellows that haven't learned the job right."

"How did you get the piece of bomb-casing in your knee, then?" Pat asked, with genuine interest.

"That would happen to a bishop," said Dan reproachfully.

Pat promised him some buttermilk and a small pig's foot to chew and went down with dragging feet to visit his other patients.

# CHAPTER XVII

There was a strangely idyllic quality in the progress of Joe and Nora in search of the boat. Blue sky, blue sea, orange seaweed and yellow-brown sand, all inset in an irregular semicircle of soft green, made an unreal and soothing effect such as we all hope to find in the next world. Everything about them now seemed so unrelated to their own way of life that for a while there was a pause or lacuna in the hitherto relentless movement towards the climax of their tragedy. As well as that, it seemed to Nora as if the largeness of the landscape about them made their own preoccupation shrink until she saw it clearly in perspective, as an infinitesimal point in history. Down on the shore a man with a horse was carting sand, slowly and leisurely, as if he knew that he was only a piece of folk-lore, a type, a person of no importance nor interest except for his occupation and the clothes that he wore, or the language that he spoke. Notwithstanding all the years in which she had been coming to Connemara for holidays, Nora still saw the people as cardboard figures without personality and without soul. There were exceptions, of course, like Sarah and her mother, and perhaps Hannah Frank. But deep in Nora's mind was implanted a conviction that she could never, in any circumstances, find common interests with the people of Connemara. To her their way of life was squalid and terrifyingly insecure, and themselves were so limited in outlook that she had nothing to say to them. She doubted if even Joe could help her to change her point of view, though she was quite willing to try. He was very often right about that sort of thing. It was one of the many good reasons why she was so fond of him. She knew that there should be good reasons, and this was why she was so distressed at Ruth's engagement to Colman, whom no one could possibly respect. It was hard to see what Ruth was getting out of the arrangement. As far as Nora could see, that kind of love was as painful as the toothache. She brooded about Ruth for a minute or two while the bright sunlight seemed to grow dark around her narrowed eyes.

"Never wallow in your misfortunes," said Joe casually. "It's the worst kind of self-indulgence."

So she kicked a stone along the sandy road and chased it and kicked it again with heavenly insouciance, until they reached the gate of Martin Faherty's house.

It was a five-barred gate of strip metal, rusty brown with age. It opened into a wide dusty yard which would be slimy in wet weather. A dozen or so of stout, elderly hens of mixed parentage squatted or strutted or pecked with an air of enjoyment, obviously undisturbed by thoughts of the soup-pot. They were like aristocrats on the eve of the French revolution. They gave the little, low, white house a somewhat raffish air. Their rank stench mingled with the scent of cabbage roses that trailed around the door and windows. The battered half-door was shut. From the black cavern above it a hearty voice called out:

"Come on in, Joeen, and bring the girl with you, if she'll come."

So, of course, Nora had to follow Joe into the dark kitchen. The old woman who was sitting on the hob did not stand up to greet them. Her seat was chosen to give her a clear view out over the half-door to the gate, and along a piece of the road so that she could see everyone passing by. She sat with her knees apart, covered to her bare feet with a voluminous red flannel petticoat, dark with turf-smoke. Her elbows rested comfortably on her knees. Her head was covered with a black and white plaid shawl crossed on the breast and tied behind at the small of her back. Her left hand cradled a clay pipe from which a cigarette protruded incongruously. Her face and hands were mahogany coloured, seamed with black.

The smell of turf-smoke masked, to some extent at least, the mixed smells of hens and cabbage-water that made Nora gasp and stretch her nostrils when she came into the room. Joe pulled out an ancient, rickety chair for Nora and another for himself, placing them both so as to derive the maximum benefit from the tiny puffs of hot outside air that came in through the doorway.

"How are you, Peggy?" he asked, in a leisurely way, as if the day were long for talk.

"Not so bad," said Peggy. "But I can't get no tobacco for the pipe and I have to smoke the ciggies. There's no bite to them. I'd as soon smoke a dock leaf. Isn't it a queer thing, now, that they'd run out of the tobacco so soon above in Fahy's? 'Tis all on account of the bridge. You heard what happened the bridge, I suppose?"

"I did," said Joe solemnly.

"And did you hear we're having a wedding?" She gave a little screech of laughter. "Our Mattie is marrying Mary Tommy on Tuesday. A tripish kind of a girl she is, not much of a hand around the house, but sure we must be satisfied. He could have got worse."

"Is Martin around the place now?" Joe asked casually.

"He's not far away. Would you be wanting him? Mattie!" she bellowed suddenly.

Nora bit her tongue in fright. Peggy waited for a moment with her head cocked on one side. When no reply came she stood up and trotted to the door.

"Tackling the ass he'll be," she said. "Let you sit there and I'll go out and find him."

The kitchen seemed unnaturally silent for a few moments after she had gone out. They could hear a soft orange flame flickering busily in the fire and the soft thud of a hen's beak on the stone of the threshold. Then very slowly the door by the fireplace opened and a young man came out of the bedroom into the kitchen. He was handsome and loose-limbed with a pleasant face in which the deep grey eyes looked too mild for a man of his years.

"I wasn't hiding," he said softly. "I was mending the straddle. I heard the old one shouting. Is she gone out into the yard?"

"She said you might be tackling the donkey," said Joe.

"That will keep her busy for a while, so," said Martin,

with extraordinary venom. "Maybe she'll take a run up the field to look for me, with God's help."

He sat on the other hob, gazing into the fire like a sick man. Nora began to feel embarrassed for him and wished she had stayed at home. However, as Joe explained why he had come, and said that Sarah had suggested Martin as a possible member of the boat's crew, the young man began to brighten up.

"Sarah is a nice girl, a real nice girl," he said with feeling. He looked up at them from under his eyebrows.

"I'll be glad to go for you. I heard the mother telling you I'm getting married on Tuesday. And I heard what she said about Mary Tommy, too. She's a one to talk about tripish, sitting all day in the chimney-corner with her old pipe, giving old talk out of her, letting the hens in around the kitchen as if they owned it." He cleared his throat loudly. Then he went on with a tumbling rush, as if he had been silent for a few weeks, and giving a long, angry gasp at the end of each sentence:

"Mary will put a bit of slacht on the place, anyway. And she's able to make a cake of bread, 'stead of going down to the shop with fourpence in her fist like a tinker woman that wouldn't have no fire at home. And she's bringing over her hens, that work for their living not like ours, and her goose, and she's promised a heifer calf. And if the mother says one word to her after she crosses that door I'll break her face for her, so I will!"

A hen tut-tutted at the door. Joe said:

"Why don't you and Mary go up and live in the mountain house for a while, until your mother gets fond of her?"

The mountain house was a one-roomed cabin where Martin could spend a few nights in the turf-cutting season.

"The mother can go up there if she doesn't like it here," said Martin. "I'm not moving a step out of this place."

During the pause that followed this last unanswerable statement, the door darkened and the old woman came trotting in again, cackling derisively:

"Ah, here's the hard man himself! Here's the big, tough, wild fellow, though you'd think to look at him he'd be afraid to pull a girl's hair."

Martin stood up noisily and shouted at Joe as if he were at the far end of a currach on a stormy night:

"All right, then. I'll come with you now over to Gander's place. We'll take his boat, I suppose."

"What boat?" The old woman hopped in between Joe and Martin, turning her head from one to the other. She thumped Martin in the chest with her fist. "You're going on no boat," she said fiercely.

"Out of me way!"

Martin swept her aside with his arm so that she danced away agilely to the far side of the room where she stood on her toes and glared and chattered like a starling.

"You're not going," she said again. "I'll get the priest after you. Striking and defying your own mother——"

A small gleam of humour came into Martin's tempestuous eye.

"Sure, the priest is on my side," he said. "Didn't he tell me I'm a married man in the sight of God now, and

I needn't bother no more with what my mother tells me? Come on, Joe. We'll be going."

Joe had already steered Nora out into the yard. She was standing distractedly among the hens, listening in terror to the shouts that were coming from the house. He put his arm gently around her shoulders and said very quietly:

"It's quite a friendly fight. They understand each other. The old woman is making her protest and she'll make it every day until the wedding is over. But she's afraid to say too much because rumour has it that her own foot slipped a great many years ago and she thinks that Martin may have heard about it."

Nora giggled.

"Dreadful of me to be so crude," said Joe, looking at her sideways out of snake-brown eyes. "I learned it from the rough soldiery."

So they all went over to see if Gander was at home. His house was built on a low rocky promontory over-looking the sea, from which it was separated only by a dry stone wall. His cabbage and potato plots were wizened from the salty spray. Even the grass around the house, though it was manured assiduously by many hens and ducks, was burnt up and bitten by the salt-laden wind. The thatch on the house was kept in place with a chignon of willow-rods which gave it a crop-eared look. The walls were thickly and brilliantly whitewashed, and a double row of round whitewashed stones led up to the front door.

The inside of the house was as pleasant as the outside. Gander's mother was there, a big, hearty, resourceful woman with a bursting romantic soul. Her husband had been lost at sea with his currach when Gander was a baby, but she was incapable of being glum for long even about this misfortune. She was always busy at dusting and cleaning and whitewashing and painting, but she was ready to stop and listen in a state of enchanted wonder to anyone that came in with a story, no matter how tame. In some respects she had the luck that often seems to go with an optimistic, happy temperament. Her house was furnished from spoils of the sea, made into tables and chairs and chests by her industrious son. Round, green and clear glass floats from French fishing-nets decorated the mantelshelf and the dresser, where also were proudly displayed no less than three sets of rosy cups and saucers which she had won, in three different years, on tickets at Toft's during Galway race week.

Gander, who was now a gigantic man of twenty-five, had acquired his nickname at the age of seven. He was his mother's only child. From the moment of his birth she had poured out on him the whole overwhelming torrent of love of which her vast spirit was capable. She appreciated to the full every move of his little body, every smallest stir of his mind, as if she were the first woman in the world ever to rear a son. Especially she gloated over his curly yellow hair, which she trained into long ringlets that trailed over his shoulders. She saw nothing incongruous in the contrast between this Bourbon elegance and the boy's scarlet, rustic face with its out-thrust lower jaw which in later life was to give him a fine, determined appearance, but which now gave him the look of a fearful, miniature Charley's Aunt.

With varying degrees of delicacy, her neighbours had urged her to have his hair cut. But she would not, she said, until after his first communion. The critics fell back at this and the dedicated ringlets were ceded a small measure of respect and understanding. It was only after the first communion was over that the long-repressed derision broke out in the nickname that he had carried ever since, and which his mother had long ago adopted herself. She had knitted him a snow-white jersey for the big day, and had also had made for him a pair of white knee-breeches, from the local báinín. For reasons of economy he had to wear these garments on Sundays for many months afterwards. He was growing quickly, and long before they were worn out he filled them tightly with his large, muscular body. They hampered his movements intolerably, so that he walked stiff-legged, protruding irresistibly at the back. The whole townland howled with laughter at the nickname. In some way not easily explained, it cleared the air of an embarrassment, and Gander had found life so much easier that he had accepted his fate almost thankfully.

Martin Faherty and Joe explained their business to Gander's mother. She sat high on a kitchen chair to listen to them, with little exclamations of horror, while she wiped her eyes repeatedly on the corner of her checked apron. Gander was down in the boat, she said, and of course he would go into Galway, and why wouldn't he? She saw them as far as the gate, murmuring sympathy all the way, and seeming so shocked that there should be such sorrow in the world that Nora felt quite guilty, as if she had confided adult troubles to a child.

The road that ran past Gander's house ended in a tiny natural harbour, a long, narrow fiord between high black rocks, covered with patches of orange lichen. Gander's hooker was moored there and he was sitting in it splicing a rope. It was almost noon. The heat of the sun was magnified in this sheltered place. They went down by steps cut in the rock and sat in the boat, lapped about with a scarifying smell of tar and ancient fish and turf-smoke, and seaweed. Martin and Gander and even Joe had been pickled in this smell long ago, so that it only made them feel comfortably at home. But Nora felt quite ill, until she remembered that Colman would have to travel all the way to Galway in this boat, in his beautiful clean clothes. This made her smile her savage, primitive smile. She only stopped when she saw Joe's eye on her.

Gander's hair still stood up in a huge mop of loose yellow curls. In spite of the heat he was wearing a high-necked, grey, jersey. While he listened to them, he went on splicing his rope with the ardent precision of an expert, bending his face downwards so as to hide his feelings, for he was almost as easily moved as his mother was. It would take an hour to prepare the boat, he said, and to bring some lambs on board—Nora was overjoyed at the prospect of another smell for Colman—and some food for the journey. He said that the breeze would be better soon, but that nevertheless they might not reach Galway before the early hours of the morning. He and Martin began a drawling, good-humoured argument about that. Presently Joe and Nora left them, promising to deliver Colman into their hands in an hour's time.

# CHAPTER XVIII

When Ruth opened the kitchen door she paused on the threshold with a sense of shock. There was no one there. She had run all the way down from the attic, certain of finding Sarah and her mother still in the kitchen, both overflowing with ready understanding and sympathy. Only the faint smell of Mrs. Lynch's bread, just beginning to bake in the oven, proved that they had been there at all. Wild unconnected imaginings shot through her mind, giving her a sensation of being attacked from many different points at the same time. This was why, when she heard a step in the passage-way behind her, she whirled around in terror and stood clutching at the kitchen door as if she were ready to dart behind it to safety. When she saw that it was Colman who was coming towards her she ran stumblingly to him and clutched at his shoulders and laid her head against the lapel of his coat, closing her eyes tightly as if she could make the whole ugly world vanish.

Colman put an uncertain arm around her and then lifted her slowly away from him as if she were a strange woman who had suddenly thrown herself on him for protection in the street. Her helplessness shocked him deeply. He had never seen her like this before.

"Ruth! What on earth——?"

"It's the man in the attic. He keeps talking about blowing things up and killing. I can't stand it. And when I came down there was no one here."

Through her half-closed eyes she hardly saw his face. Again she rubbed her forehead against his chest. He spoke very low, into the top of her head. His breath tickled her through her hair.

"Ruth. Come with me on the boat. Come away from all this. Into Galway. I insist. You shouldn't be here. You're not needed. And they don't want you. If they did someone would have been here waiting for you."

"The Connemara men would never allow a girl to go on a boat. They think it brings bad luck."

"I bet Joe Thornton could persuade them."

This time Colman made no attempt to conceal his genuine contempt for Joe. His tone brought Ruth a little to her senses, so that she realized that she had actually been examining Colman's proposition seriously. She moved away from him and looked up at him without speaking.

"Do come with me," he went on urgently. "It's our only chance. It's awful here. This is no holiday. It's doing something terrible to you. You're always so calm. I can't stand it."

Ruth asked, without expression:

"What about the babies?"

"It's Sarah's job to mind them. Not yours. No one could expect it."

"I don't believe that. Besides, I couldn't leave Nora. It wouldn't be proper."

"There are plenty of old hens here to look after Nora's morals. That sort of thing doesn't matter in a situation like this. Can't you see? You should be with me. They're expecting me to persuade a doctor to come out here in the boat. I won't be able to do it. I know I won't. You could help me. You've never failed me before. I can't get on without you. I feel now that I'm surrounded by enemies. You think I can't see that they all hate me. You should be on my side, against them, and you're not."

"Of course I'm on your side," Ruth protested.

Again she was seized with the same helpless terror that had sent her running down from the attic. Great, deep waves of it went through her. There was a dreadful, heavy rhythmic pounding, coursing right through her body, as a drowning man must feel in the last moments before he gives up fighting for breath. Then, like a sudden lifebuoy, came a small quiet sign of returning control. She experienced, for the first time in her life, a feeling of irritation with Colman. She did not recognize it at first as her salvation. She only knew that she no longer wanted to burst out into childish wails, and throw herself on the floor and cling to Colman's resisting hands and implore him to stay with her, to be good to her, to look after her and protect her from the horrible realities that pressed all around her. Irritation diverted her attention. Colman's reaction to her heartbroken appeal fitted into a commonplace pattern. It was as if she had complained of a headache to someone who immediately and querulously explained that himself was afflicted with a worse one. Always until now Colman's troubles had appeared to her on an heroic scale. Now, very faintly in the depths of her mind, an idea began to form that on the contrary they were small and a little mean, and that some integral defect in Colman's character was the cause of them. From this notion another sprang easily, that as each problem was settled, he would always manage to produce a new one, and her task in Colman's life would be to go on settling these petty problems for him till death did them part.

Just now, however, she had no more than a glimpse of this. With a reassuring sense of returning power she said:

"It's nonsense to say that everyone is against you. If they were, why would they turn to you now for help?"

"To get rid of me," said Colman, with the fearful perspicacity of a self-engrossed man.

"Nonsense!" said Ruth again. "They would never think of such a thing. You're looking for insults." She stopped suddenly, for she had not meant to let her new insight show. She hardly recognized it yet, herself, and she knew that she must take it away and examine it in secret, like a man who has found a buried treasure on his land, before deciding what was to be done with it.

Fortunately, Colman was considering her last statement with the care that he gave to everything she said concerning him.

"I expect you're right," he said. "I suppose one naturally becomes over-suspicious from being badly treated."

Ruth thought of his large house, his motor-car, his

yacht, his factory, and even in the midst of her distress she could not forbear from giggling.

She quoted:

> "*Happy the man whose wish and care,*
> *A few paternal acres bound,*
> *Content to breathe his native air,*
> *In his own ground.*

"Did you know that Pope was only twelve when he wrote that stuffy little piece? He hadn't time to learn much about contentment. And a fat banker, called Rogers, has another one: 'Mine be a cot beside a hill——' "

"I don't understand you when you're like this," said Colman fretfully. "Please don't laugh at me. I didn't say I'm short of money."

"No," said Ruth. "You did not."

She closed the kitchen door carefully, thinking of the bread in the oven which must not be in a draught. Then she said:

"If you're going to be in the boat for part of the night you should bring a heavy jersey with you. It will be cold enough for that."

"Yes, I brought one along in case there would be any sailing."

"I'll go up and help you to get your things together."

So when Nora and Joe came back to say that Gander's boat would go in less than an hour's time, Colman was all ready for them, even to having Mrs. Lynch's hot new loaf wrapped up in a cloth, filling the drawing-room with its aromatic steam.

At the first sight of the house Nora's feet had begun

to drag. The intermission was over. Now her inconvenient conscience reproached her for not having been sufficiently miserable during the last hour. So the moment that they reached the hall she started towards the little room at the back of the house. Pat met her in the dim corridor.

"Where are you going?"

"Down to see the babies."

"No, no. Sarah is with them. Come back and tell me about the boat."

He took her arm and steered her back to the drawing-room. She glanced at him sideways, wondering if she would insist on having her own way, but his look of absent-minded determination prevented her.

In the drawing-room Joe was already telling Ruth and Colman about the boat. Nora sat as far away from Colman as possible and took no part in the conversation except to say that Gander was going to bring some lambs for cargo. When the others began to talk of going down to the quay she stood up and said:

"I'll just go along and see if Sarah wants anything."

"No," said Pat. "Don't do that. We'll all go down to the boat together. The more of us there are the better. It will make Martin and Gander hurry when they see how anxious we are."

"Wouldn't it be a good thing if Sarah came, too, then?" said Nora. "And Gander will hurry anyway. He said he would."

"For heaven's sake, Nora, don't make difficulties," Pat said sharply.

Nora looked at him in astonishment, but before she

could reply Joe was across the room and leading her out into the hall, saying over his shoulder to the others:

"Come along, everyone. Take your provender, Colman. We'd better go quickly before Captain Horgan stops us."

They went in a solid little group, down the avenue and out on to the white, dusty road. Nora hung back a little at first, hoping that Ruth and Colman would walk out in front as they usually did. But this time they showed no signs of breaking away, and after a moment Joe took Nora's arm and made her keep pace with the rest.

"I'm tired," she complained in a low voice to Joe. "And it's so hot. I wish Pat would have let me stay behind."

"I expect he had his reasons," said Joe cheerfully. "It's not far."

Martin Faherty saw them from over his own half-door. He came out to the gate to head them off in case they had intended to call at the house for him.

"Wait there," he said firmly. "I'll be out to ye in two shakes."

So they waited under the grilling heat of the sun while the little cloud of flies that was travelling with them intensified their intolerable buzzing and darting. They could hear the voice of Martin's mother, monotonously angry, rattling out an unending stream of abuse. Presently Martin came out of the house, shutting the half-door slowly and carefully behind him like a man in a daze. He joined their group without a word. All the way to Gander's little pier he kept his head lowered and his eyes on the ground.

Gander's headland was alive with small, mountainy black-faced lambs. His mother was helping the dog to keep them from running back along the road, flapping her arms and her wide skirts at them and hooting like a sea-gull. In a moment Gander and Martin were catching the lambs, throwing them on the ground and then carrying them down the stone steps to the boat where they huddled in terrified submission. The men did it so efficiently that it did not occur to the others to offer help. They sat on the short, springy grass among the ticking insects, while Joe gave Colman exact instructions about finding a doctor and describing the infants' symptoms. Pat took no part in this. He lay on his back, supporting his head on his interlaced hands and gazed out under half-closed eyelids at the pale blue, gently moving sea, as if he were on the point of falling asleep. Nora found herself glancing at him again and again. There was something in his behaviour that reminded her of a man who thinks that he has cracked his skull in a fall and is now afraid to move quickly lest he may injure himself fatally. Combined with this there was a new look of maturity and detachment that seemed so strange to Nora that it filled her with panic. Yesterday she would have shouted her fears aloud and demanded an explanation, and complained of people who made mysteries and secrets. But now she only edged a little nearer to Joe and tried not to stare at Pat hard enough for him to notice it.

Presently all of the lambs were shipped. Gander's mother came over, panting and sweating as if she had had to do the whole of the work herself.

"There's some fine fat little lads there," she said

proudly, looking down into the boat. "There's great atin' on a fat lamb."

Her hearty, friendly eye encountered Colman's cold uninterested one on its sweep around the group. She recoiled at once into an unusual shyness.

"I'll be going home now," she said in a hurt tone. "I wish ye a safe journey and God speed ye." She whirled around to call down noisily into the boat: "Hoi, Gander! Get a good price for them lambs, or don't come home no more!"

Ruth sprang up immediately and walked with her as far as the road which she had to cross in order to go home. The old woman thanked her emphatically for this attention, taking Ruth's hand in both of her own and trying to convey her gratitude without admitting in words that there had been any need for it. When she had gone Ruth did not go back to where Joe and Nora and Pat now stood high on the headland looking down into the boat. Instead she went down the stone steps with Colman and stood close beside him while he handed his bundle to Gander. Then, as Colman was about to climb on board, she took him by the shoulders and turned him towards her, while she looked up into his face with a long, calm scrutiny as if she were fixing something in her memory for all time. The two Connemara men turned away quietly and became very busy with ropes. Colman found himself stirred throughout his being with mixed sensations of pity and panic. Very softly, he said:

"Won't you come with me, after all? There's still time."

"No."

He hardly heard her. It seemed as if at the moment of speaking her voice refused to obey her. He could feel her whole body shake against him. Her face was dead white now. For one awful moment each understood what was in the mind of the other. Ruth swayed closer against him. He called out roughly:

"Joe! Come down here and look after Ruth!"

Joe was down the steps in a second. He took Ruth step by step up on to the headland, holding her so firmly that she felt strength flow into her from him. Only when she was standing beside Nora did she turn and look down at the boat again. It was already cast off and Martin and Gander were easing it out of the little harbour with boat-hooks, while Colman fussily tended the mainsail.

Nora was astonished at the sight of Ruth's desolation. This was something quite beyond her understanding. If this were love, she thought, then her own calm attachment to Joe was something quite different.

"He'll be back in two days," she said desperately.

No one answered. She wished she had said nothing for now she felt that she had been childishly tactless. The boat was outside now and filling with the south-westerly breeze that had sprung up since noon, as Gander had predicted. Still they stood there as if there were not a thousand reasons why they should hurry back to Derrylea. Glancing across towards Gander's house, they could see that his mother was standing motionless as themselves at the gable, watching until the boat became a black speck, like a fly on a pale-blue ceiling.

Joe was the first to move. As soon as the boat had

173

passed completely beyond hailing distance, he turned his back deliberately on the sea and said:

"Now, Pat."

Pat moved his head a little, painfully. Very slowly he began to walk down the grassy slope and out on to the road. The others followed him silently. When he stopped after a few minutes and leaned his back against the sunny wall that bounded the road, they stood in front of him in a tiny semicircle. Then he told them that Paul was dead.

# CHAPTER XIX

Nora said sharply:

"No! He can't be." She took a step forward and glared at Pat. "Are you sure?"

"Yes. I am sure."

"I guessed it," said Joe.

What hurt Nora more than anything else was the one slow tear that Joe could not suppress. Unnoticed by him it rested on his sharp cheek-bone until it dried in the sun. In a thin, small voice Ruth asked Pat:

"Did Colman know about this?"

"No," said Pat wearily. "I don't know if I did right in letting him go without telling him. But I was afraid that if I did, the boat would be delayed in starting. There is still Jane to think of." He sighed with a heavy, rasping sound. "And I was thinking, too, that Colman is not really a member of the family yet, and perhaps it would be unfair to burden him with our troubles. I'm sorry, Ruth. It's hard to think clearly."

Ruth said:

"It's all right, Paddy. I think you did right." She paused for a moment to search for words in which to ask her next question. Then, hesitantly, she said: "When did it happen?"

"While you were upstairs with Colman. Nora was still out with Joe, seeing about the boat. I came down from the attic soon after you left it, when I had finished bandaging the man's knee. Does anyone know his name?"

"I think I heard someone call him Dan," said Joe gently.

"Dan. Well, it doesn't matter. I went down to see the babies. Sarah and her mother had just come in from the kitchen. We told Hannah Frank that she could go home for an hour. After she had gone we were looking at the babies, and Paul gave a little whine. He just shivered once and I think he died then."

At this all of Nora's feelings became condensed into a black bitterness that shocked even herself. The directness and honesty of her nature left her completely defenceless against the impact of tragedy. She saw it in every detail, with appalling clearness. She envied Ruth her preoccupation with Colman, which must mask to some extent her feelings about Paul. Above all, his death appeared to Nora as a monstrous injustice. For her, his clear, humorous innocence had been his principal charm. She had to blame someone.

"That Captain Horgan." She stammered in her eagerness. "It's his fault. If there had been a train to Galway we could have brought the babies in there when they got sick first."

Suddenly she remembered the fly in the milk and hence her own part in the child's death. Her mouth opened and she clapped her fingers against it to keep in the words that would betray her. She looked at Joe with horrified eyes. He said:

"It's no use blaming anyone. If Paul had been ill for a week or more, there would be some sense in it. Surely no child could die of gastro-enteritis in two days."

"Unless he had a congenital heart," said Pat. "I've been thinking and thinking about it. I can see no other explanation. There's something in one of the books about those babies. They live about six months, sometimes longer, or until they get their first severe illness, and then they die."

For one second Nora was almost jubilant with relief, until she remembered that Paul was dead. Dead. Until now the word had meant hardly anything to her. Now it had to be examined as if it were a word that she had never heard before. Ruth was saying sharply:

"What about Jane? Perhaps she is the same?"

"I don't know," said Pat flatly. "They're twins."

He heaved himself off the wall and they began to walk distractedly along the road home, each of them desperately trying to come to terms with misfortune. Ruth said presently, into a sickly little silence:

"How are we going to send word to Aunt Margaret?"

"I'll go for Father Regan," said Joe presently. "We'll have to have a funeral."

"No, no!" Nora exclaimed. "I can't bear it!"

She stamped away to the side of the road and shook her hair down at either side of her face to hide her tears. No one answered her, as no one had answered Ruth.

The thought of the child's mother had completed their conviction of personal failure. No amount of explanation could rid them of it. Each of them carried it like an impossible burden which could never be laid down: the sheer physical effort of it kept them silent and preoccupied until they turned in through the gateway of Derrylea House.

Before they were half-way up the avenue they became aware of a far-off sound of wailing. Nora stopped, but Joe at her elbow pushed her forward again. The sound became clearer with every step they took until it was recognizable as the long, undulating, high-pitched, wordless song that is the keen for the dead. Instead of being wild and primitive as it often was in this place, it expressed a lonely, sad resignation which penetrated deep into the bone and shivered through their being.

"It's Hannah Frank," said Joe, in a tone of fury. "I'll stop her."

He darted up the steps. They could hear him plunging away towards the back of the house. Then the wailing stopped and sanity returned. They followed Joe with heavy slow steps into the house, oppressed already with thoughts of the things that must be done.

At three o'clock in the afternoon Captain Horgan came into the kitchen while they were trying to eat a late meal there. The yard was as silent as a hospital corridor. The men whispered and walked on tiptoe, apparently seeing nothing incongruous in their pity for the dead child, side by side with their own relentless acts of war. Only a faint rustle came in through the open door. Ruth, Pat, Nora and Brian were there. An hour ago Joe had gone on a borrowed bicycle to the curate's house, four miles away. Sarah could not be separated from Jane. She sat in the little room watching her fiercely as if she could protect her by mere vigilance. Mrs. Lynch and Hannah Frank had approached Ruth together, and asked her if she would approve of their using her parents' bedroom for Paul.

" 'Tisn't because he was only a baby that he shouldn't be laid out decent," said Hannah Frank, a little aggressively, as if she expected that Ruth would not do the right thing.

Ruth said:

"I'm afraid I don't know anything about what should be done. Would you please take charge?" She appealed to Mrs. Lynch.

Hannah told her that they had holy candles and a child's habit which had been got years ago for one of her own daughters who was thought to be going to die of the typhoid, but who was now safely grown up and working in Boston.

They promised to call Ruth and show her the result of their work as soon as they would be ready. She forced herself not to run as she left them to join the others in the kitchen. She could not bear to be alone now, not even for a few minutes.

Captain Horgan sat in a vacant chair at the table without waiting to be asked. He looked around from one of them to the other, and finally addressed Ruth:

"I'm heartily sorry for your trouble. It was to be, I suppose. We didn't hinder you from getting help, anyway."

179

He lowered his head and looked up at her from under his heavy black eyebrows.

"We know you didn't," said Ruth gently. "We don't blame you at all."

Horgan seemed pleased at this. He went on, more briskly:

"We'll be pushing on, this evening." He glanced quickly at Brian and away again. "We'll wait for the darkness, of course, because we must bring Dan on a stretcher. I was up with him just now, and mind you, he's telling the truth, all right, when he says he can't walk."

"If he had been injured anywhere but in the knee——" Pat murmured.

"Sure, I know," said Horgan. " 'Twas bad luck, and no mistake. And a very valuable man he was, too."

He smothered this last statement in a growling cough. There was a little silence, full of embarrassment. Into the middle of it came Joe, looking curiously haunted, or frightened: until now it was he who had seemed best equipped to deal with each problem as it arose. He dropped into a chair at the table as if the eight-mile bicycle ride had been too great an exertion for him. He folded his hands on the table and examined them with intensity as if he had never seen them before. Then he said, carefully modulating his voice to an everyday level:

"Father Regan is away in Galway. His housekeeper says that he went on Wednesday morning, meaning to stay the night. Wednesday was the day we came, the day of the cattle market, the day the bridges were blown up.

180

She hasn't heard a word from him since. She says he'll surely find a way of coming back to-morrow night, so that there can be Mass on Sunday morning."

"This must be Friday, then," Ruth murmured, surprised.

Pat said:

"Can we wait until Sunday?"

"Wait for what?" Nora asked stupidly.

"We needn't discuss it now," said Joe quickly, but Pat said, in the new, flat tone that had not left him since he had told them that Paul was dead:

"For the funeral. It's no use trying to get out of it."

"Perhaps we could wait and see if Father Regan manages to get back to-morrow night," said Joe.

"The weather is too hot," said Pat.

Nora laid her head down on her arms and wept. Joe glared at Pat and said furiously:

"Have you no sense at all? There's no need for the girls to listen to this. You seem to be trying to make it as unpleasant as possible."

"Am I? I don't know. I'm just saying what I think."

"Well, don't."

He stretched out a hand mechanically and stroked Nora's hair. Horgan said:

"I'd send a man over to Carna for a priest, but that we must be going in the opposite direction at the fall of night." He spread his hands apologetically. "I wish I could do something for ye."

Brian said:

"The priest in Carna is very old. I don't believe he

could come. And his horse is old, too. It's twenty-one miles."

Now through the open doorway they heard a rhythmic murmuring that stopped and started and stopped again.

" 'Tis the men saying the rosary for the little garlach," said Horgan. "I came in to tell ye about it, and to say, would ye come and join in? They'd like it if ye would, because it would show ye don't bear them any grudge."

Ruth stood up at once and said:

"Of course we will."

She led the way out into the yard. The shadow of the house cut it in half. Just out of the sun the sleepy hens were gathered in soft bundles. The air was so still that newly-shed feathers lay without moving on the cobbles. A faint steam rose from the hen's drinking-trough, an unsavoury vessel from which, Norah always thought, no one but a hen would be foolish enough to drink. The men were kneeling in rows on the flagged floor of the coach-house nearest the back door of the house. Led by the singer of yesterday, they were praying in Irish, with the intensity of deep, unshakable conviction. As he moved in among them with the others, Joe was reminded of all the places in which he had prayed for dead comrades, in wet graveyards and dusty halls, in theatres and in churches. Now it seemed to him that he recognized the same tone in the men's prayers for Paul, as if he had been elected an honorary martyr of the revolution. He noticed that Mitey's Irish rolled out with the authentic accent of the Achill Island, and not with the strange foreign one that he used in English.

Early in the evening, long before it was dark, the neighbours began to call. Cáit Conneeley was the first. She took two huge soda-loaves from under her best brown shawl and laid them on the kitchen table.

"I thought ye might be short," she said shyly. "There's currants in one."

She began to help Mrs. Lynch to arrange chairs by the walls and to lay the table with a white cloth, and cups and saucers, and huge plates of her own bread and butter. Ruth stood and watched them helplessly. They made it plain, without words, that it was not her place to be hostess at the night's celebrations, that this was a neighbour's task. Hannah Frank fussed in and out, and presently she took Cáit away upstairs to show her that everything was in order there. The moment that they were out of the room Ruth ran to Mrs. Lynch and seized her arm.

"Are they really going to make a wake of it? For a baby?" she whispered.

"Sure, you can't stop that," said Mrs. Lynch soothingly, though she was clearly a little shocked. " 'Tisn't often nowadays that we'd have a wake for a little baby, but they want to have it for a compliment to your father and mother. Besides 'tis a good way to pass the night."

"I suppose so."

It was too late now to wish that she had not revealed her feelings. And the visitors were a comfort, in a way. All the faces were so friendly that even Nora had to soften her bitter mood for their sake. Gander's mother came, of course, and presently, ludicrously trying to

183

hide behind the others, an obviously reluctant Kate. Word had got around that it was not the fever after all, and in any case she could not afford to be absent on such an important occasion. She had paid a shilling for a dozen clay pipes at Fahy's shop and she had also brought some tobacco from a private store of her own because, as she said, she knew that there was none in the shop. In this way she hoped to re-establish herself as a friend of the family. She sat partly concealed by the open kitchen door, taking no part in the preparations for supper and peeping out now and then to see if Sarah had come into the room. She kept her shawl on, in spite of the heat, so that she would be able to disappear into it whenever Sarah would come, and her great, black, ostentatious rosary beads were ready twisted around the fingers of her right hand so that at any moment she could become preoccupied with her prayers.

As the visitors arrived they were brought upstairs to the room where Paul lay in state, surrounded by Hannah's holy candles. Everyone knelt by the bedside to say a short prayer, and then moved back to sit for a few respectful minutes on the chairs that stood with their backs to the wall. All night long people would keep coming up to the bedroom, so that Paul would never be alone. The old women exclaimed delightedly at his beauty and then wept because he was dead.

Back in the kitchen the men sat at one side and the women at the other. Once they had tiptoed into their places the men replaced their wide black hats squarely on their heads, reached for the already filled clay pipes and began to talk about the progress of the potato crop, and the state of the fishing, both of which were bad on account of the long hot spell. Then they talked about the turf harvest, which was good for the same reason.

Gander's mother settled herself more comfortably in her chair and said it was a pity that there wasn't an open fire, because it would be more homely looking. The fire glowed fiercely through the bars of the range, and was replenished often throughout the night from the big turf-basket that stood near by. When the daylight grew dim Mrs. Lynch lit two oil-lamps and hung them one at either side of the fireplace. Then she got out two tall bottles of poiteen and measured out a good glassful for each of the adults, who immediately took a small drink and said:

"The blessing of God on the souls of the dead."

Pat and Joe had some, but Ruth and Nora refused. They had all tried sitting in the drawing-room, but they had soon given it up. There was less time to think in the bustle of the hot, crowded kitchen.

Several children were there, including three of Cáit Conneeley's. They took the handing around of drinks as a sign that the atmosphere had lightened, and one by one they began to come out from behind their parents' chairs. Cáit's son Peteen took up his stand in front of the fire, facing the room. He was fourteen years old. But for his knowing expression he might have been only ten. He wore a furry grey tweed cap, several sizes too big for him, slanted towards one ear. His feet were bare and his grey toes twitched with excitement on the warm flags of the floor. His knee-breeches, of grey glasheen-caorach,

185

hung slackly down to the middle of his shins. From under his loose grey jacket he took a short thick ash-stick. He pointed this fiercely at the nearest boy to him and said:

"Casabianca!"

"Ay, sir," said the boy.

To the next he said:

"Niagara!"

"Ay, sir!"

"Jack the Ripper!"

"Ay, sir!"

When he had given one of these queer names to each child, he whirled the stick in the air, gave a little skip on the floor and started off on a high, chanting note:

> *"The priest of the parish went out one night;*
> *He lost his most considering cap.*
> *Some says this and some says that and some says——"*

He gazed at each member of the trembling group in turn and then suddenly pointed his stick at one:

"Niagara!"

A rapid dialogue followed:

"Is it me, sir?"

"Yes, you, sir!"

"You're a liar, sir!"

Then there was a piece of unintelligible mumbo-jumbo from the other boy, interspersed with sharp inter-jections, intended to confuse, from Peteen. Nervous at being the first choice and the centre of attention of a ring of adults, inevitably the boy broke down. Then Peteen had the pleasure of giving him several wicked blows on the legs with his stick. Deeply satisfied, he glared around at the now-mesmerized semicircle of his adversaries and started again:

> "*The priest of the parish went out one night;*
>   *He lost his most considering cap——*"

"Peteen is the divil painted," said Martin Faherty's mother admiringly.

She sat in the nearest place to the fire on the women's side of the room, her elbows on her knees, darting black-beetle glances around at everyone to make sure that she was not being slighted. She was very dirty, but the woman who sat beside her would not have dreamed of edging away, lest she might give offence.

Slightly elevated by the poiteen, some of the younger men joined in the next game, though they still left Peteen in charge. He broke off a small piece of turf from one of the sods in the basket. This was passed from hand to hand, each time with a little piece of dialogue:

"Take this."
"What's this?"
"A fat hen."

The little piece of turf was passed on:

"Take this."
"What's this?"
"Two ducks and a fat hen."

Thus an item to be remembered was added each time. When anyone broke down Peteen's stick came into action and then they started all over again. The game finished with Michael Folan, a young man of about twenty, who had had Peteen's position until he had become too old for it, intoning with his head thrown back and his eyes half-closed:

> "*Twelve bulls in a bull-field roaring,*
>   *Eleven monkeys in their chimney-corners smoking,*
>   *Ten blacksmiths on their anvils beating,*
>   *Nine ministers in their pulpits preaching,*
>   *Eight crooked crows with their crooked toes in the*
>       *crooked crab-tree creaking,*
>   *Seven grey mares well shod and shorn,*
>   *Their tails and manes in very good order,*
>   *Six piggericks in a rye-field rooting,*
>   *Five grey geese in a green field grazing,*
>   *Four hares headless,*
>   *Three plump partridges,*
>   *Two ducks,*
>   *And a fat hen!*"

He was congratulated vigorously. People recalled that he had always been a great hand at the poetry when he was at school. They said that the brain was there, and you couldn't do much without it.

Ruth knew that very soon they would begin to sing bitter old songs whose sweet haunting airs would only intensify their sadness. Even while she thought of it, Michael Folan was standing up, closing his eyes tightly and reaching out both groping hands to be held by a friend on either side of him. All chatter stopped while he began in a strong, true, rhythmic, tenor voice:

> "*Young Emily was a serving-maid,*
>   *Her love was a sailor bold.*

*He ploughed the western main and got*
*A large amount of gold."*

Throughout the sad story of Emily, while her cruel
parents were creeping into the sailorman's room at night
and murdering him for his gold, Ruth was saying over
and over inside herself:

"Thank God, thank God, thank God Colman is not
here!"

# CHAPTER XX

At intervals throughout the afternoon and evening Ruth and Nora went to sit with Sarah in the little room. They found that, as usual, she was more concerned for them than for herself. She knew that there was a wake in progress and she was afraid that this would upset them.

"They'd never think of having a wake if your father and mother were here," she said. "But it would be a lonesome sort of a thing to have none, all the same."

Ruth said:

"We don't mind. It's always better to do the proper thing."

" 'Tis, I suppose," said Sarah doubtfully.

She had not been able to think clearly since her mother had taken Paul away. At intervals of a few minutes she became possessed with a terrible, irrational conviction that she was urgently needed somewhere else, but always when this message reached her conscious mind, she knew that it was an illusion caused by the fact that Paul had passed beyond her help. Then she would jump up in fright and peer at her remaining charge, and drop back, immeasurably relieved at finding her still alive. Sarah was shocked at herself for behaving in this animal fashion. She knew that lack of sleep was partly responsible for it, but she had no intention of remedying this.

Ruth said, looking into the cradle:

"She's not getting any worse, I think."

"She keeps on looking around for Paul."

Then Sarah wished she had not said this, though it was quite true, because it seemed to make things worse for Nora. She was glad when they went away. Everything she said in her confused state seemed to hurt them. She liked it better when Joe came. With him she did not dissolve into near-hysteria as she did with the girls. And she had more respect for his judgement. When he said that Jane was not getting worse, she had to believe him.

After one of these visits Joe went out through the front hall on to the steps to breathe the still night air. He was quite accustomed to wakes. When he was a small boy he had always been one of the little crowd of children who slipped in and out between the adults, making the most of the rare evening's entertainment. His father had never allowed him to join in the games, however, and he still retained a prejudice against them. Perhaps it was the thought of the games as well as the discomfort of the hot, tobacco-laden air that prevented him from going straight back to the kitchen now. Besides he needed a little time to himself. His brain seemed to have slowed down in a curiously unpleasant way. This meant that no sooner had he worked out one problem than several more had piled up, so that it seemed as if he would never succeed in coming to the end of them. It reminded him of that horrible little problem of the snail which climbed up one inch of a pole every day and then slipped back two inches. He knew that he must sleep some time to-night. Otherwise to-morrow would be impossible. A great, grey fog settled over him at the thought of to-morrow.

Very slowly he walked along the little sandy avenue that ran by the side of the house. There was a grove of cypress and fir and holly there, bordered with a low hedge of tiny, strongly scented roses, whose blooms were pale yellow and pink in the daytime. Now in the strong moonlight everything was etched in black and grey.

Where the avenue ended at the big double doors of the stableyard, he watched dark figures of men begin to slip out, one by one, through the wicket-gate and over the stile into the paddock beyond. Their guns and baggage gave them strange bulky shapes. Strongly and bitterly Joe remembered the feel of these night movements, when you were filled with a special affection and warmth towards your comrades, so that even death seemed easy. "Wrap the green flag round me, boys," in fact. Though he hated this war with a savage hatred, still he could not help feeling a pang now as if he were being excluded and left behind against his will.

Suddenly, half-dazed as he was, he recognized a familiar boyish figure among the others, light and slim and straight like every MacAuley that ever was, and swaggering a little under a long, clumsy rifle. Instantly Joe's interest in his own troubles vanished. Wide awake now he began to run along the path, calling out softly as he went:

"Brian! Wait a moment!"

He thought it possible that Brian would skip over the stile and disappear into the darkness. But he turned at once, as Joe realized now he would inevitably do. Before Joe reached him, Horgan came out through the wicket-gate and shut it carefully behind him. Then, disregarding Joe who was now no more than a yard away from them, he took Brian's elbow and began to walk briskly towards the stile.

"Wait a moment!" said Joe again. "Where are you going, Brian?"

Horgan stopped and said quietly:

"Don't raise your voice. He's coming with us. We need every man we can get."

"Man?" said Joe. "He's only a boy. Take your hand off his arm. This is a nice return for hospitality, I must say."

"That means nothing to me," said Horgan, "because I'm no gentleman." They measured each other. "And what age were you in 1916, anyway? Did anyone tell you then that you were only a boy?"

"That was different. That wasn't civil war."

"I don't see what that has to do with it," said Horgan. "It's a question of judgement. Brian is a free man and well able to make up his own mind."

"Stop talking about me as if I weren't here," said Brian calmly.

He eased himself out of Horgan's grip and said, carefully, as if he were weighing every word:

"I'm sorry you saw me, Joe. That was bad luck for both of us. It would have been easier for everyone if you had just found that I was gone. I did leave a letter on my dressing-table."

"But why are you so anxious to go?" Joe asked desperately. "You can't want to be mixed up in a civil war."

"Can't I? I don't see it as a family quarrel, as you seem to do. I think the mistake you make is in thinking that the war is over, that's all. In every war there is a right moment to stop. That Treaty should never have been signed. I believe what Captain Horgan says, that you can't build on rotten foundations."

"I know the Treaty shouldn't have been accepted," said Joe patiently. "But civil war is a worse affliction than a dishonourable treaty. And at least the British have left the country."

"The seven devils that were in them have entered into the Free State Army," said Horgan.

"You keep out of this," said Joe hotly.

Horgan shrugged and said:

"Come along, Brian. The men are waiting."

But Brian still spoke to Joe.

"I don't see much of a change in the country since the British went," he said. "And they're not all gone, either."

"There won't be any miracle," said Joe. "It takes years to build a new state. You must wait ten, twenty years. Then you'll see changes. We'll get them all out in time."

"It's risky," said Brian. "I'd rather see the starting-point more secure. It's easy for you to talk," he burst out, after a moment's pause. "You were in it at the best time. I was ten years old. That's a ridiculous age. My blood boiled. I was as useless as a cat. But I'm not useless now. I'm able to carry a gun like anyone else. There are several people of my age in this very column. This is my chance to do what I can for Ireland, and I'm going to take it. You should understand that."

The passionate, childish words filled Joe with despair, for he knew that argument was useless. Only by physical force could Brian be restrained now, and even if Joe would have tried this, Horgan was there to prevent it. He shifted his ground.

"Have you thought of how your mother will feel?"

"She's not likely to understand," said Brian without expression, but the tremor in his voice betrayed him. "It won't mean very much to her. You see, she's protected from most nasty things, because she never sees them as they really are. Look at what she did to Ruth, urging her to marry that great self-centred bully Colman. He tormented her as long as he stayed here, and then disappeared at the first sign of trouble."

"Disappeared? Nonsense. He's only gone into Galway to get a doctor for the baby."

"You'll see he won't come back," said Brian, no longer able to keep a note of hysteria out of his voice. "And she'll be hurt even more. She'll feel disgraced. My mother should never have allowed it. She *wanted* Ruth to be married. She *wanted* her to go away and live somewhere else. Can you imagine anyone feeling like that about Ruth? And what makes it so much worse is that Ruth hangs on every word my mother says. She only wants to please her. She wants to please everyone. She even wanted to please Colman."

"Supposing you're right about Colman, that he's not coming back," said Joe, "aren't you doing the same thing? Aren't you running away, too?"

"I'm going away," Brian corrected him, "that's a very different thing. I don't want to be here when Ruth discovers what Colman has done. In any case she won't notice whether I'm here or not. I'll tell you something." Horgan made an impatient gesture. "It's all right, Captain. This is the end of it." He turned back to Joe. "Paul is dead. I hate that. It's cruel and ugly. Do you know that no one told me about it? Do you know how I found out? I heard Hannah Frank raising the keen over him. I'll remember that always. I heard her, and I went in, and there she was, swaying up and down and wailing. The room was dark. Sarah's mother was there, too. She came over to the door when she saw me and she told me about it. She showed Paul to me. It's time I went away, because I must think out why no one told me. Pat knew at that stage."

"Pat wanted Colman to go on the boat before telling the rest of us."

"But he didn't make sure that I was there when he told you. No one told me about any of the things that happened. Well, I didn't mind that. But Paul being dead was different. That changes everything."

"It was your own fault that you didn't know what was happening," Joe pointed out. "You didn't stay with the family. You were always going off by yourself."

"That's true. I haven't blamed anyone, did you

notice? I used to feel mean and wicked when I went off by myself. I knew there was nothing wrong in it, and still I felt guilty. Now I can see quite plainly that that was stupid. I'm not just one leg of a centipede. I don't have to move every time the main body wriggles along. I'm a separate person."

To a MacAuley, Joe thought, this discovery was likely to be a shock. In the closed in, protected air of that household, neuroses grew fat and overbearing and un-manageable. Things that were simple everyday truths to a countryman like himself, were to a MacAuley vast and terrifyingly tempting wastes to be explored and charted painfully, with many scrapings of the con-science. Even now Brian was explaining further:

"Don't you see that once I know all this I must go away with Captain Horgan? I knew before now that I should go and fight on the Republican side. But I let a feeling of responsibility to the family stop me. Now that's no longer necessary, since I see that the family doesn't feel responsible to me."

At this Joe said woodenly, hardly trusting himself to speak:

"Run along, sonny, and join the army. You'll learn a lot of things, I can promise you. Come back and tell me some of them later."

As Horgan swept Brian away over the stile Joe ran across to call softly after them:

"Look after him, Horgan, for God's sake!"

"I will," came Horgan's voice out of the darkness jeeringly, "and you can look after Dan!"

As he watched them flit across the little paddock, Joe

reflected on the misfortunes of possessing an Irish conscience. Unless Brian's youth were to save him, it seemed certain that he would join the ranks of those scrupulous amateur soldiers who had once killed a few men and who felt as a result that they could never again look their God straight in the face. They were spiritually allied to the other type, that would let a spy escape as soon as he raised the question of the future of his wife and children.

"And look at me," thought Joe, "crawling up the walls because I must read the prayers for the dead over Paul to-morrow. Too much imagination is the curse of all the Celtic races."

He turned in through the stableyard to tell Pat that Brian was gone and to verify his conclusion from Horgan's parting remark that the column had decided to leave their wounded man behind them in the attic, after all.

# CHAPTER XXI

Towards morning even the young people at the wake began to get sleepy. The older women had long ago begun to doze intermittently in the comfort and privacy of their shawls. Only the fact that their rosary beads stopped moving through their fingers betrayed them. The old men did not sleep, except for Patcheen Phaddy who was eighty-seven, and who leaned his head against the wall and snored gently and rhythmically with his toothless mouth open until Michael Folan, who was sitting beside him, poked him into silence. The other old men sat rigidly upright, talking in lower and lower tones and at less frequent intervals until at last they were silent altogether. The little boys lay in heaps on the floor, resting their heads on each other's bodies like pups. In sleep, their faces had lost the wicked, clurachan look and had become innocent and pathetic again, so that their mothers watching them felt moved to forgive them for their latest devilment.

At four o'clock the cocks in the yard began to crow, but it was six before Hannah made tea for the second time. There was no member of the family present now, so everyone was able to relax and enjoy the meal. Ruth and Nora had gone away to bed at two o'clock, Nora protesting that she would not be able to sleep.

"Rubbish," said Joe shortly. "People can always sleep, if they want to."

Then he and Pat went into the drawing-room and built up the fire, more for the sake of its appearance than for any need of its warmth. Almost casually, for he was too tired now to be diplomatic, Joe described his conversation with Brian. Pat said:

"How long ago did this happen?"

"Half an hour ago. Just before I went into the kitchen to tell the girls to go to bed."

"Then it's no use my going after him. I'd never find him now."

"It would have been no use even if I had told you at once," said Joe. "Two minutes after they left me they were out on the bog. And they've left us their dynamiter in exchange. I rather expected that. You can't go into battle carrying a man on a stretcher, as I explained to him just now."

"Into battle? Do you know where they're going?"

"Towards Clifden. They have designs on the barracks there, I'd say. You'll just have to put Brian out of your mind until you see him again."

"That's not so easy," said Pat drily.

"I told Horgan to look after him."

Suddenly Joe was asleep. Pat sat and watched him for a while, but he showed no sign of waking up. Persecuted by his thoughts, at last Pat stood up and began to walk jerkily about. As Joe did not move, presently he left the room, closing the door softly behind him, and went up to the attic. He made Dan's bed and bandaged his knee, but he could do nothing to comfort him in his desolation at being left behind by his captain. He lay there, allowing Pat to minister to him, with his eyelids down like shutters over his brooding, dark eyes. When he spoke at last it was to ask Pat if he would arrange to-morrow to have him brought on a sidecar to his own house in Carna where, he said, his sister would look after him. He went to great trouble to explain that he meant no disrespect to Derrylea House, and that in fact his sister was a sour old jade, but that since they had enough trouble here already he thought it would be more fitting-like for him to go home now. He was so earnest that Pat promised to see Roddy Folan about it, and then he wandered drearily downstairs again to find Sarah.

It was Mrs. Lynch who was with Jane, however. She said that she had sent Sarah to bed. She steered him over at once to look into the one remaining cradle.

"Joeen Thornton told Sarah that this one is getting better," she said, watching Pat's face anxiously to see if he agreed. "She drank a fine bottle of goat's milk there a while ago and it don't seem to have done her no harm."

Jane was sleeping quietly now, though her face still looked worried and old. He warned Mrs. Lynch not to feed her too often, and went back to the drawing-room to doze and dream in an uncomfortable armchair.

He awoke in the warm sunlight to find the ritual still going on, laceratingly impersonal yet soothingly traditional. Someone had made a little white coffin, which it seemed was the proper thing for Paul. Everyone went to visit him and pray for him again, passing and re-passing each other stumblingly on the unaccustomed stairs. Pat and Joe had breakfast with Ruth and Nora in the dining-room. It was only at the end of it that Ruth said suddenly:

"Where is Brian? Did no one think of calling him?"

Pat and Joe looked at each other guiltily, realizing now that they should have awakened her last night and told her that Brian was gone. Then the dim candle-light would have helped to create a mood in which Brian's action would have been in some way understandable. Here, in the glowing light of day, it was just another failure, and thus it reproduced in Ruth and Nora the almost intolerable pain that they had experienced at the news of Paul's death, and which they had each thought could not possibly be repeated with the same intensity.

They came to terms with it because they must. Nora said:

"I knew he was up to something, but I couldn't make out what it was. How are we going to persuade people that we couldn't have stopped him?"

"We're going to be very busy if we start justifying ourselves. I think it will be much better not to try."

This from Ruth was so bitter that the others looked at her in astonishment.

"It's like being shipwrecked," she went on softly, half to herself, "watching people all around you drowning."

"Brian would have gone away even if his parents had been here," said Joe firmly. "He would have found an excuse. Nothing would have stopped him. I know the signs."

"Will he get killed?" Nora asked in a rush, knowing well the foolishness of the question.

"If he does, it will be his own business," said Joe. "I didn't."

Mrs. Lynch came to the door then to say that if they were ready the funeral should start, because the men must go to work afterwards. Consulted by Joe she agreed that it would be quite proper for Ruth and Nora not to go to the funeral, but that they should come upstairs to say one prayer instead. Nora almost refused, but she managed to control herself in time. Escorted by the young men, they went up to the darkened room where the shortened candles still burned and the air was heavy with their waxy smell. The old women, crouched at their prayers by the walls, murmured in little bursts of sympathy as the girls knelt beside the bed. They did not know that Nora's eyes were tightly shut against her spread fingers. Ruth felt compelled to look, however, to make sure that Paul was properly dressed and lying comfortably in his white coffin. Then she was caught unawares by a great fountain of tears that seemed to spring from the depths of her heart. Her head went down on to Hannah's best starched white bedspread, which she had loaned for the wake. Pat took her out, and downstairs to the drawing-room. As she went she heard the old women giving sharp exclamations of pity. It seemed to her that they sounded a little scandalized, too, and she was sorry for it. Still she knew that their philosophy allowed them the paradox of being scandalized without disapproval, so that they would not hold her weakness against her. She wished that she could be like Nora, who had cared far more for Paul, but who was now able to sit upright and still as death while they listened to the funeral procession shuffle through the hall. Nora knew her own mind; that was it, thought Ruth.

Nora knew her own mind. As soon as the trains were running again, or perhaps even before that—Joe would fix it—Nora was determined to leave Connemara for ever. Clutching her fingers to prevent them from jumping about, she was thinking that when this house would crumble away and grass would grow up between the flagstones on which her feet now rested, when every one of the ignorant peasants who had made a night's amusement out of Paul's death was as dead as he, she would not care. She would be glad. She wished she could be like Samson now, and pull down the house on top of them before they could get out on to the sunny steps, before their feet would strike precisely on the gravel, walking so carefully because of their important burden.

Suddenly she stood up and went to the window. In a second Ruth was beside her. Together they watched the procession move across the gravel on to the avenue, headed by two huge men who shouldered the tiny coffin between them as if it taxed their strength to its limits. Behind them came the old women waddling busily in their shawls, and then the men, in loose formation. The old men trotted, holding themselves upright with one hand under the tails of their coats, needing two or even three steps for every one taken by the younger men.

Then Nora caught sight of Joe. He was walking with Pat close beside him, but still Pat looked as if he were alone with a group of strangers. A moment or two passed before she understood why she retained this impression. It was because Joe belonged so completely with the Connemara men. All unconsciously he had slipped into their way of walking, with short, springy steps as if he were out on a mountain-side. He was at ease with these men in the special way that is only possible between people who have been young together. As a small boy Joe had been at school with the men of his own age here. The older men had taught him to fish and sail a boat, had brought him turf-cutting and hay-making and had let him ride on their horses. He had done all of these things as one of themselves. When Pat went out in one of the fishing-boats, it had been as an honoured stranger with whom familiarity could never go beyond a certain point.

Now that she saw this Nora knew that she must not hate Joe's country and his people. She must not call them ignorant peasants. They were his oldest friends. They knew him better than she did, in some ways. And he would bring her back here often, after they were married. That was always Joe's way. He had said before, more than once, that the world must not be dotted with black spots covering the places where you could not go because something nasty had once happened there. It would be no use just pretending to like Connemara and raging against it inside, because Joe always knew what she was thinking about. She would not have been surprised now if he had turned his head as the procession began to pass out of sight around the bend of the avenue and had sent her a sharp warning glance that would strike through the glass of the window. She drew Ruth back into the room, out of the sunlight, and they looked at each other helplessly. Then suddenly they both thought of Sarah and went to find her.

Joe was engrossed in the business of walking steadily. He wished he were old, like the old men who walked so determinedly with one hand under their coat-tails and who had seen so many funerals. For one moment a wild hope seized him that one of them might read the prayers. But even if they remembered how to read it would be no good because their eyes were dim and their heads dreamy. He knew that it would not be possible to persuade one of the younger men to do it. They would insist that such a specialized task be undertaken by one or other of the men of learning present. To ask Pat was out of the question, though he seemed more wideawake to-day.

In spite of the trend of his thoughts, Joe had his Missal ready in his pocket. He knew quite well that there was no escape for him. He did not intend to protest. To do so would be a hitch in the smoothly-running ritual. Everyone would be upset by it, all these good neighbours who had left their beds last night and their work to-day to have a full-dress funeral for a six months old baby, though babies were cheap in Connemara.

The graveyard was only half a mile away. It was approached by a steeply-mounting, grass-grown lane whose high, close stone walls cut off the view of the country-side around. At the top of the lane there was a rusty gate with a stile beside it. Most of the people went over the stile, but the coffin was carried through the

206

gateway. The graveyard was a wilderness of giant nettles and docks and tall grasses heavily weighted with seeds. Here and there pathways had been mown. Some of the families kept their graves in good order with their small headstones erect. But others were careless and there the grass grew rank and wild, and the stones had fallen askew. Scattered everywhere without any pattern there were little mounds which were graves. Each of these was marked with a single uncarven stone half-buried in the grass, lying in wait to trip unwatchful feet. No one knew who owned these graves, though it was said that most of them dated from the famine times, Black '47 and after, when funerals were so plentiful that they ceased to be interesting.

At the upper end of the graveyard Saint Finnian's oratory stood four-square and roofless. The grass was always short here because Saint Finnian had built on a platform of stone which even now, after thirteen centuries, was only lightly covered with soil. Still the inside of the oratory was full of nettles, through which all the people would walk barefoot, praying and doing penance on the Pattern Day in August.

Opposite the door of the oratory, as near to it as there was depth of ground, the grave was open. Pat saw it in a dream. He had no idea of the night-long discussion and argument about the exact place where Paul should lie. The rights of everyone for yards around must be respected. It was felt at last that Saint Finnian would approve of this choice because he was fond of children himself. Indeed, if he had been asked for help in time, the old women said, Paul might not have died at all. And as soon as Father Regan would come back from Galway they would bring him up to bless the grave and approve of it, too.

Listening with half of his mind to the murmurings around him, Pat marvelled at Joe's assurance, and his knowledge of the course that things must take. At the right moment he even had an open Missal in his hand and was sprinkling holy water into the grave with a cypress twig supplied by Roddy Folan. Then he began to read aloud in a clear, calm voice, dropping the words into the still, hot air, like pebbles into a summer pool:

"Let us pray. O God, whose nature it is ever to have mercy and to spare: we suppliantly entreat Thee on behalf of the soul of Thy servant Paul whom Thou hast this day bid to pass out of this life; deliver him not, we beseech Thee, into the hands of the enemy, nor be Thou unmindful of him forever: but command that he be taken up by Thy holy Angels and borne to our home in heaven: that having put his faith and trust in Thee, he may not undergo the pains of hell, but obtain the joys of everlasting life, through Christ our Lord."

"Amen," said all the people standing around the grave.

Joe flicked over a page quickly and then read:

"Eternal rest give to him, O Lord, and let perpetual light shine upon him. May he rest in peace."

"Amen."

When the grave was half full of earth Hannah Frank threw herself suddenly on her knees and burst into piercing wails which gradually resolved themselves into the keen for the dead. She swayed up and down, throwing her clasped hands out in front of her. No one took any notice, except that the two men with the shovels worked a little faster. She kept it up without a break until everyone had said a private prayer and had gone away down through the grass and over the stile into the lane. When she was sure that the last person had gone, she stopped wailing. She stood up, arranged her shawl tightly around her and straightened her long back. Erect and steady she marched down to the stile, crossed it swiftly and set out for home, darting sharp looks to left and right as she went.

# CHAPTER XXII

It was two days before the boat came back. A calmness, like a paralysis, had descended on the house after the funeral was over, so that no one talked of the future. Kate was back in the kitchen cooking food that was more to her employers' liking than to her own. This was the only sign she gave that her self-confidence was diminished. She seemed also to have achieved some small flicker of understanding of Sarah's personal sorrow, for she forbore from inviting her, as she was longing to do, to confidential speculations about the reactions of Paul's mother to the news of his death. She sighed often but comfortably as she went about the kitchen. Out in the yard, killing cocks in the ashpit and plucking them in a sunny corner, she sang very softly to herself to keep her heart up. She was sorry the men of the column had gone away without saying good-bye to her.

Ruth stayed with Sarah in the little room for most of the time, hardly talking at all, helping her, bringing her trays of food, sending her out for half an hour now and then. Together they watched while Jane grew visibly stronger and more childlike in appearance.

Nora walked with undisciplined fury for hours each

day, accompanied by the patient and philosophical Joe. When she threw herself on the grass at last, miles from home, he was always at her elbow with a parcel of sandwiches which she ate voraciously. He always knew a man with a sidecar who lived near and who would be willing to drive them home. She went to bed exhausted each night, but her sleep was slashed with screaming nightmares.

Sitting alone in the drawing-room on the evening after the funeral Joe and Pat congratulated each other on having got rid of Colman, who would have been unbearable if he had been here now.

"But I'm afraid we may have got rid of him more thoroughly than we intended," said Joe.

He told him of Brian's certainty that Colman would not come back. This possibility had obviously never occurred to Pat. He rubbed his hands together in a little swift movement of delight.

"Wouldn't that be perfect——" He stopped suddenly. "Ruth. It will be an easy escape for her, if she can only see it that way. God knows I tried hard enough to like Colman. But he's so *bone-headed*."

"I think I'll warn Nora not to burst into cheers if he's not on the boat," said Joe. "I wonder if Ruth half expects this to happen."

"You think that Colman may have told her?"

"No, no. He would never have had the courage to do that, poor fish. I just think she may have guessed it. Remember her manner when he was going away?"

"Then how did she bear the wake and the funeral? How did she bear them?"

Presently Pat broke through what seemed like an aeon of silence to ask humbly:

"Joe, what effect will all this have on Ruth?"

"I was thinking of something I saw once in Galway," said Joe. "There was a fall of snow early in June. It was caused by icebergs floating in the Gulf Stream, several hundred miles out to sea, someone said. The roses were in flower. I saw them covered with snow. They looked like frost flowers on glass. When the snow melted it hadn't injured the roses. I think it will be like that with Ruth." He paused to watch Pat for a moment. "I've always hoped that she would not marry Colman after all. She would never have tolerated him for so long if she didn't have some special quality of heroism. Very inconvenient. Makes you put up with all sorts of impossible people."

"I can't think clearly about it yet," Pat complained.

"Then don't try," Joe advised him. "For all we know, Colman may be on the boat when it comes back."

But he was not. Gander's mother came running in, red-faced, on Sunday evening, to say that she had sighted the hooker out at sea. How she had recognized it was a mystery. When they all hurried down to look it was still only a black speck moving leisurely in on the indolent breeze. The sea had time to turn from blue to grey before the boat was near enough for Gander and his mother to start hooting to each other. Two other figures were visible, one at the helm and the other standing motionless amidships. The old woman peered, and then turned excitedly to Joe.

"It's Father Regan, and he'll be heartbroken over

having no Mass for us this morning. There must be no sign of the train yet, or he wouldn't be coming this way. But they haven't brought the doctor after all, and sure maybe it's just as well with the baby getting better on her own, God bless her, and the little lad gone to heaven. You'd scruple to bring a doctor out this far and then to have to tell him he wasn't needed after all."

It was this misplaced meekness that left them all in the hands of that scoundrel Kenny, Pat thought absent-mindedly. He was watching Ruth. She had moved away from the others and had gone to stand on the highest point of the headland where it was undercut by the sea. From here she was able to see down into the boat as it passed into the little rocky harbour. The priest looked up at her and waved a cheerful hand, but the other two affected to be too busy. When the boat had moved in out of her sight, she turned quickly and came down to say to Pat:

"I'll go back to Sarah now."

Then she was running down the grassy slope, out into the road. They watched her until she slowed down to a swift walk.

Gander's mother was waiting down by the steps when the boat came alongside. She caught the rope that her son threw to her and tied it neatly to the single bollard. The three men came ashore at once. Joe went a little way down the steps to say:

"Well, Gander? What happened?"

Gander looked anxiously upwards to where Pat and Nora stood at the top of the steps. Then, relieved at seeing that Ruth was not there, he said in a low voice:

"Come up to the house and I'll tell ye all about it."

"I'll be going home," said Martin Faherty in a loud, determined tone. "The mother will be expecting me."

His two days of freedom seemed to have restored his manhood. Joe hoped that his mother would observe this quickly and let him alone.

At her house Gander's mother was already laying the shiny oilcloth-covered table with the best cups and saucers when the rest of the party arrived. She had prudently hung the great, black, dusty kettle on the crane over the fire before going down to meet the boat, so that she had come back to find the water boiling, sputtering through the spout into the hot ashes. Though she had not expected the honour of giving tea to the priest, she had a sultana soda-loaf ready. She always had plenty of milk from one or other of her two Kerry cows. That was the best of having two cows. If one was dry, then you could nearly always be sure that the other was not, and you need never be going over to the neighbours with an apologetic tin can hidden under your shawl. Indeed, it was usually the neighbours that had to come to her, and that was much nicer.

As she made the tea in her huge and unique china teapot, which she would have defended with her life, if necessary, she listened to Joe tell Gander and the priest about Paul, how he was dead and buried, God rest him. She was afraid that the priest would ask if there had been poiteen at the wake, for he was dead against it, for some reason. But he seemed to have got such a shock that he was hardly able to say anything. She chose this good moment to pour the tea. Father Regan was only the same age as Gander, so she was able to say to him:

"Pull over your chair now, a-mac, and eat up. 'Twill put life in you after the journey."

To herself she added the hope that it would take his mind off the poiteen.

Almost before she had finished pouring Joe said again, impatiently:

"Well, Gander? What happened?"

"I'd like to speak plain," said Gander slowly, looking directly at Pat and Nora. " 'Tis not a nice story."

"Just go ahead, Gander," said Pat. "We've all guessed at part of it already."

"Have ye, now? 'Tisn't easy to tell it, all the same. The big fellow hardly opened his mouth all the way into Galway. Mind you, he's a good man in a boat, without a doubt. The two of us noticed that he got kind of excited-like when he got in near Galway, and he began gathering up his baggage and putting it down again, and hopping from one end of the boat to the other like a sea-gull. We went over to the Claddagh side, thinking we'd slip in there and get a bit of news from the Claddagh men before we'd go ashore. But, mo léar, we never got ashore at all. Out came a little motor-boat, and soldiers with uniforms and guns as long as pikes. They took all the lambs from us, Mother, without a penny payment. They said Michael Collins will pay for them some day, but I'm thinking that'll be the long day."

"What harm," said his mother impatiently. "Go on. What happened then?"

"Then they said we were to turn around and sail back

where we came from. Mr. Andrews said he demanded to be let go ashore. At first they wouldn't listen to him, and then they seemed to get an idea that he might be someone important and they began to talk between themselves about what they ought to do. When the big fellow heard that, didn't he start gabbling about how he couldn't stand it out there in the back of Connemara with children sick in the house so that the place was like a hospital, and a gang of thugs and gunmen camped out in the yard, gloating over the damage they done to the railway. The soldiers were terrible nice to him when they heard that. Man, they handed him ashore like he'd be the Queen of Sheba. Two of them walked him up the docks between them, and we didn't see him no more."

"Did he tell them that he had come to get a doctor for the children?" Pat asked without expression.

"He did not," said Gander, stirring his tea expertly with the forefinger of his right hand. "He was kind of excited, as I was saying. I told them myself, and so did Martin, but sure, they wouldn't take no notice of the like of us. Father Regan, here, tried them too, but it was no use. He was down asking the Claddagh men if one of them would sail him home, on account of there being no train. After a lot of arguing he was let come with us. We had to up sail there and then and start back. The little motor-boat followed us nearly as far as Barna to make sure we wouldn't slip in again. That's the very thing we were planning, too. You'd think they knew it, so you would."

"Perhaps Colman really meant to get the doctor," said Nora in a subdued tone. "Perhaps he came back to

216

the docks later and was surprised to find that you had gone."

"Ah, no," said Gander kindly. "Just before he got off the boat I asked him, quiet-like, was that what was in his mind, and I said I'd wait for him no matter what happened. But he said he wasn't coming back no more and he offered me a pound note for his passage on my boat. I said no, thanks, and he might be needing it himself on the rocky road to Dublin."

"Oh!" said his mother, shocked.

" 'Tis hard to be mannerly all the time," said Gander with resignation. "You don't think I'd have taken his dirty money, do you?"

"No, no," she murmured, "but he's such a fine-looking gentleman."

"That's only the outside of him. Inside he's just a mean little rasper."

He drank some tea delicately.

Pat walked home alone to tell this story to Ruth. He found her in the drawing-room stroking Joanna, the cat, on her lap. Like all cats, Joanna was willing to make capital for herself out of human misfortune. Being blessed by nature with a comforting fur coat, she always presented herself for petting in moments of tension. At first Ruth showed no surprise. Then, deliberately brutal, Pat told her in Gander's words how Colman had spoken of the children, and how he had quite unnecessarily given away the secret of the column in the yard.

"He's done us a pretty bad turn," said Pat. "Brian is with that column. Of course Colman didn't know that, but he was asked not to talk about it and still it was the first thing he mentioned. The Staters will probably be out here on lorries during the day."

Ruth stood up with a jerk so that Joanna had to spring resentfully to the floor. Then, without a word, she ran out of the room. Pat shrugged and lay back on the sofa, suddenly tired of handling other people's affairs.

Ruth walked quickly down the avenue and out on to the dusty road. She knew that Sarah's mother was at home now, catching up on her neglected housework. With vague resentment she wished it were not so hot. Already her hair lay in damp streaks on her forehead. The low sun blinded her, too, especially while she was running up the hilly lane to Mrs. Lynch's house. When she stood on the doorstep she was breathing quickly and unevenly. She knew that this was a danger signal. She must keep her head, at least while she was talking. One hysterical fit breeds another, she was thinking; I can't trust myself any more.

Mrs. Lynch dropped her hands into the basin of bread that she was kneading at the kitchen table. Quickly she scraped her fingers clean against each other and went to open the half-door and conduct Ruth into the kitchen.

"I must get into Galway somehow, at once," said Ruth sharply. "You can help me."

"Why? What do you want in Galway?"

"I should have gone with Colman on the boat. He asked me to."

"Is the boat back?"

"Yes, half an hour ago. He doesn't get on well without me."

Her voice shook, in spite of her. She dashed away the first tear impatiently.

"And he didn't come back on the boat?" Mrs. Lynch asked shrewdly.

Ruth shook her head. A moment later she was in the old woman's arms, leaning her head against the little shawl that smelled of turf, being stroked like Joanna and led over to the rocking-chair by the fire.

"You're not going into Galway," said Mrs. Lynch softly. "You're well out of him. You're not going running after that fellow as if there wasn't another man in Ireland for you."

Ruth looked at her, miserably disappointed and wondering where she could turn now for help.

"I'm thinking you haven't a notion of what it's like to be married," said Mrs. Lynch dispassionately. "Mr. Andrews is a fine-looking man, I'll say. But he's kind of puffed-up in himself. I wouldn't like to have him around the house morning, noon and night. In a little while he'd be telling you he didn't like the food you'd be giving him, and how he saw a cobweb on the staircase, and that the children had no manners and the maids weren't doing their work right and 'twould all be your fault. He'd be a grouser. 'Tis in his face, God help him. And you'd have to ask his leave before you'd do every little thing, which would be a queer state of affairs because he's a stupid class of a man, and 'tis you that have the brains. And he'd blame you if a child got sick or died, God between us and all harm. A fat lot of sympathy anyone got from him when there was trouble in the house below. Of course I'll grant you he'd think a lot more of his own child. That class of a man is always very careful of his own property."

"Then wouldn't he be careful of me?" Ruth asked, suddenly stimulated into amusement.

Still she resisted a little the delightful temptation to let Colman carry the burden of his stupidity alone. Mrs. Lynch said:

"He would not, then. You'd be like a person that would be working for him, and nothing you'd do would be right."

Ruth made her last faint protest:

"Surely you're being too hard on him."

"I am not," said Mrs. Lynch with certainty. "I saw the like of him in New York. You're young enough to forget him. 'Tis a fine thing to be young, sometimes."

She went back to her bread. As Ruth silently watched her neatly forming the loaf and putting it to bake in the pot-oven on the hearth, for the first time she began to see that after the events of this week nothing could be exactly the same again. She wondered if it was recognition of this that had made Brian go away. A new phase had already begun in the lives of all of them, even of Sarah. It was impossible to hold it back. Already she knew that Paul had begun to move into the past; he would return often without warning to trouble her, like a forgotten embarrassment, but he would never deliberately be recalled.

# POOLBEG

## The Lilac Bus

### Maeve Binchy

By the best-selling author of
*Light a Penny Candle* and *Echoes*.

A collection of eight interwoven tales, brimming with wit
and laughter. The people who travel on the Lilac Bus
lead separate lives in Dublin during the week, but are
thrown together at weekends for the journey home to
Rathdoon. Their paths begin to cross in an unexpected
and intriguing way.... In these stories, Maeve Binchy
uses deft touches of irony and humour to point to the
goodness and folly of human nature.

ISBN 0 905169 78 6

Rep of Irl IR£3.50
UK£3.15

# POOLBEG

## Truth in the Night

### Michael McLaverty

In *Truth in the Night,* considered by many to be his finest
novel, Michael McLaverty returns to Rathlin Island, the
scene of part of his first book, *Call My Brother Back.*
Whereas in that book the island is seen with the uncritical
eye of a child, here it is viewed more realistically.
Although its beauty is evocatively portrayed, life on the
island is clearly hard – too hard for some people: the
Craigs, who soon abandon it for Belfast; and Vera Reilly,
the sharp-tongued unhappy mainland woman, widowed
with one daughter who longs to leave. The story of her
second marriage to Martin Gallagher, a native of the
island whose return after a long absence signifies the
fulfilment of a lifelong dream, is told with compassion but
unflinching realism.

The character of a tightly-knit rural community, with its
concern for its own and suspicion of the stranger, is
magnificently conveyed. Rarely in a novel has the
redemptive power of love been more manifest.

ISBN 0 905169 72 7                    Rep of Irl IR£3.95
                                              UK£3.45